When Malibu, after the sun goes down, retains a ﹍﹍﹍-but-not-quite dark blue aura, the sea loses its greenish tinge, the beach empties of players and bathers, the breeze floats in carrying salty mist, the tide appears to have reduced its force, gulls squawk louder, patio chairs squeak as oceanfront dwellers sit to gaze thoughtfully toward the blackening horizon, it (Malibu) exists in a moment lost, intangible, precious, fixed. History buries itself behind, tomorrow awaits ahead, the moment becomes lost as it extends (for it has no past, no future, no link to any other time, only an isolated, transitory existence in fading blue), shortly extinguished as the blue becomes so dark it isn't blue, it's night. Night engages another realm, of dinner, drinking, watching TV, studying books, conversation in person or on the phone, anything except that "moment lost," after the sun goes down, before the night grabs hold -- a new realm generally rich in activity, rather than reflection, of partying, not chair lounging, of games with the kids, channel surfing, putting dishes in the washer, clothes in the dryer, curtains across the windows, jokes ("did you hear this one? A panda walks into a restaurant..."), arguments ("God wouldn't deliberately

create us as sinners...") ("what do you mean by 'surrender'?"), twisted pronouncements ("if you really cared about me you'd let me see him/her once in a while"), reckless decisions ("maybe so, but I'm going to lie about it..."), hardy reinforcements ("I told you you'd make it big, didn't I?"), and weak-kneed fables ("probably everyone wants to do it, come on, admit it, you do too"), dressing up to go out, or pumping iron, aerobics, stair-climbing, yoga, etc., etc., if the will is there. If not, the internet or the DVD or the card game or the movie in the screening room in one of the fancy beach-fronting abodes. But the moment lost has been lost once again, like the girlfriend/boyfriend last year, or farther back than that, twenty-five years ago, or the agent's client who went to another agency, or the missed opportunity, the rejected proposal, the job pass-over, the tricky financial deal that went bad, the freedom relinquished or the entanglement escaped. Blue precious Malibu, Tad's dream.

He'd experienced that pre-evening moment lost, had convinced himself it would be his some wonderful day, all his, each day, not simply via visiting, but by owning, or at the least, renting, a big house on that special beach. All Tad needed was the money, and the fame (what good is

that moment without the fame?), and he'd relax in a deck
chair before the darkening horizon like a king. Or a
prince. Getting into that position was the chore. Finding
the path to that position was the arduous task facing him,
a task doubly difficult due to his plan to be an artist, to
propel himself to the top without the aid of, as they say,
crass, cheap commercialism.

Getting into "Hollywood" was easier than Tad
predicted. And significantly more easy than his mother had
warned -- in fact, she'd tried to dash his hopes entirely
by saying it would be too hard for him, the implication
being while <u>some</u> can make it, <u>he</u> certainly wouldn't be good
enough to. Nevertheless, for the final performance of his
college play (his second year of, but third year at,
college) Tad had invited his high school drama teacher, who
brought another former student, who had been a year ahead
of Tad, whom the high school teacher had sent to Hollywood
to meet an old friend (of the drama teacher's), a casting
director, who'd auditioned the former high school student,
liked him, and sent him out on job interviews, acting jobs,
one of which the former student (Zack) succeeded in
"landing," and he began, gradually, to find more jobs in

the TV series guest-spot niche. Zack was impressed with
Tad's performance in the college play, and did what the
teacher had done for him two years previously: sent Tad to
Hollywood to meet the casting director, who auditioned Tad,
who liked Tad, who sent Tad on job interviews. He didn't
get hired as quickly as Zack (a robust, smiling 6-foot-2
powerhouse) but was "signed" with Zack's agent, who
eventually found him work. Easy. No more college, no more
college plays. An apartment with another wannabe star, a
black actor he met on a TV job, a two-month stint as a
clerk at Blockbuster, a three-month part-time stint as a
sales clerk at "Murray's Fashions," and Tad landed his
first feature film role, leaving small guest parts on TV
behind.

It was not a large part (seven lines, including a:
"Look out!") in a low-budget horror movie, but yet Tad felt
the story spoke artistic nuance by questioning the purpose
of life amid modern gadgetry. Can humans keep trusting one
another when a malevolent scientist creates an implant
which takes over the bodies of normal medical personnel in
a big city hospital? And the remote-controlled staff
(including doctors) lure unsuspecting patients into the

implant room for "treatment," turning them into robots of the same type? Tad's role was a young newlywed trying to save his wife from the implant surgery, but who gets killed by a non-human nurse with large breasts. His bride survives, however, and the scientist is arrested along with the robots. The answer: yes, people will still care about others, even while doubting their humanity.

First day of filming Tad had a scene with his "wife" in the emergency room -- she had a twisted ankle sustained in a fall while running on the beach during their honeymoon -- but the majority of the conversation was between his "wife" and another "patient." She is led off to the doctor as the scene ends. Later that day Tad was photographed (filmed) pacing up and down a corridor, looking worried, glancing at the clock on the wall. The director told him to look more worried, so Tad imagined his wife was in labor. He felt the exaggerated facial expressions were not appropriate, but, after all, it was a horror movie. He asked the actress playing his wife if she wanted to have a bite to eat after filming, but she said she had to get home to her family. So he ate at Carrows, as usual, by himself.

When Tad returned to his apartment (really a small house connected to five others in an old Hollywood complex with a yard between two rows of bungalows, grass needing water, roofs needing repair, gate broken and open into the street), Sam his roommate was out, so he had no one to tell of the experience. Unless he called his ex-girlfriend Sara, which idea proved, upon reflection, not sufficient motivation. She'd ask more questions than he felt like providing responses to, like: did you have to kiss the actress? And, will you call me when the movie comes out? And, how much are they paying you? And, who else is in the cast that I might know? Brad Pitt?

So he looked through the pages of his remaining scenes, watched the news, gave up waiting for Sam, and went to bed.

On the set at the hospital the next day he was introduced to Amanda, who was playing a robot nurse. They talked outside her dressing cubicle, Tad finding her sweet, deep eyes almost, if not more, provocative than her humungous breasts. They were to work together later that day. They ran lines, one-half page of them, and she excused herself, climbing the three steps to her open cubicle, waving, stepping in, closing the door gently.

Tad walked to the food table -- "Craft Service" -- and found nothing he wanted. Screams issued from a corridor on the ground floor of the hospital -- a rehearsal. The lunch wagon, which served up breakfast early in the day, had closed down, but he got a coffee from the dispenser, always functioning, near the end of the wagon. He could hear cooks' voices inside, but saw no one because the front aperture was shut completely. He went to his dressing room and sat on the stairs before it, sipping the coffee. He heard more screams from the hospital, saw male crew members carrying pieces of equipment in and out of the entrance. There was one tall, thin female crew member who kept her eyes down as she passed Tad. He wondered what her job was. Lighting? Camera, or, rather, "focus" puller? Wardrobe? Hell, she could be one of the producers, for all he knew, except she was not dressed up enough. And seemed too shy. Her jeans were old, with holes in the knees -- although perhaps she bought them that way. So many cables went into the hospital entrance, running on the ground, that the double doors could not close at all. Two small sandbags with cloth handles propped open one of the large doors. He smiled at two of the men but they were so busy they could only nod and hurry on. It was overcast, around 70 degrees, no wind, vague traffic sounds from a distance, and frequent calls of "Quiet! Rehearsal!" emitting from the doorway. At length an even sterner warning came out, repeated by a young production assistant with headset, about 30 feet from Tad, to the effect that real shooting of film was imminent. Then "Hold the work!" and "Rolling sound!" and "Roll camera," whereupon all outside work stopped, the crew suddenly standing or crouching down still, like an atomic bomb was dropping, and silence. Something was happening inside, obviously, but Tad heard nothing. Then, those screams. Then a crashing noise, like a table turning over, a couple of loud yells, then: "Cut! Going again!" hollered from the doorway, repeated by the production assistant, and the frozen crew members suddenly began working, joking, moving gear, reaching into boxes, walking every which way. It didn't interest Tad.

Amanda came from her dressing room -- that interested him. She walked, with her cell phone to her ear, toward Tad's perch, looked at him with those dazzling eyes, said: "My God! Who was it?" into the phone, passing around the end of the dressing room trailer out of sight. It felt weird that she was to be killing him with an electric gizmo later that day. She didn't look like a crazed robot murderer. In fact, she hadn't read her lines all that well, he recalled, forcing him to the conclusion she'd not been hired for her acting ability. Maybe it was her first job -- except she wasn't at all nervous. He felt more nervous, inside, than she looked, on the outside. He'd have to ask her, at lunch perhaps, if he could overcome his shyness.

But at lunch she wasn't around. Instead the 40ish female sound engineer sat beside him, her tray loaded with food, all but yelling, "Hello, Tad! What's up?"

"Nothing," he responded. "Haven't done anything yet."

"They're running a little behind," she laughed, eating a forkful of salad. After hardly chewing, she added: "<u>Always</u> late, this company. My third film with them." She ate more salad and glanced around the table at the others.

One small man in a black cowboy shirt nodded agreeably. His thick eyebrows belied his soft, high-pitched voice: "Sure, always late, always slow. I'm Preston, by the way," holding out his hand to Tad. They shook, Tad wondering if the man was gay, because he held his hand a bit long, smiling at Tad like a friendly puppy.

"Tad Walsh. Glad to meet you. Are you in the cast?"

"Me? No." He made a face, placing his fingers to his cheek, turning toward the side, slightly, looking overly serious, as though performing an acting moment, and laughed. The woman laughed, too.

"He's the set designer. Haven't you all met?" Before anyone responded a perky blonde teenage girl sat beside the woman, placing her tray on the table. "Oh, Fanny! Where were you all morning?" the woman asked.

"I got up late, sorry."

"This is Francine. I call her Fanny, which she hates!" She laughed, putting her hand on Tad's arm. "Here's Tad, the actor. And Preston, and Jan --" indicating the wardrobe assistant beside Preston. All said hellos.

"Can't we call you Fanny?" Tad asked, feeling aggressive because of her big smile.

"Please, let's," Preston intoned.

She faked a charming pout, shaking her head 'No.'

The sound engineer laughed loudly. "My niece. Only I get to call her Fanny."

"Nice to meet you, Francine," Tad said formally, eliciting more laughter than he thought his remarks warranted. They all ate quietly for a minute, until Francine asked Tad what other movies he'd been in.

"Oh, a couple," he lied. "You never heard of them. I worked on stage, mostly."

"Really? I'm doing a play right now. *THE TEMPEST*?" She smiled that big smile.

"I can guess which role," he said, in a sort of conspiratorial manner, knowing the play, knowing the young girl's part which fit her.

"Oh, you do?"

"Yes. Good part for you. At school?"

"No, Redland Playhouse. In Upland. Equity theatre," meaning professional.

"Shouldn't that be 'Upland Playhouse'?"

"No, haven't you ever heard of it?"

"Sorry," he replied. "I haven't. When do you start?"

"It's already started," the woman interjected. Tad wished he remembered her name. Too late to ask her now. "You close in one week, isn't that...?" She looked at Francine, who said:

"Yes," and to Tad, "Will you come and see me?"

Later, in costume, in makeup, his hair combed and sprayed, his shoes too tight, Tad waited outside the hospital mouthing his words. The overcast sky had cleared, permitting afternoon sunshine to warm up the location considerably. Amanda was still in the hair and makeup trailer, while another actor, a black kid named Shaun, sat with his parents near the wardrobe trailer, which was actually one-half of a unit also used as the "extras" dressing room. Shaun didn't seem too happy, and his stern mother, in a chair beside him, was whispering in his ear. Tad guessed she was telling him not to be nervous. The father, sitting on the other side of Shaun, ignored them both, reading *Newsweek* magazine.

Amanda sprang from the trailer, resplendent in tight candy striper outfit, low-cut beyond reality, hair a burst of red -- a wig, hiding her brown hair. Too much makeup, Tad concluded, but it was none of his business. She was led by a serious-looking second assistant to the hospital door, his voice crying into his headset mike: "I'm bringing her in right now. We're walking in now!" Shaun looked up, rose from his chair, and stood watching. Then immediately the second assistant returned, calling: "First team!" to Shaun and Tad. Not exactly the same escort

Amanda had. The two actors entered the building. Tad put a friendly hand on the kid's shoulder, but there was no response. His parents followed.

Inside, past lighting equipment, cables, the thin female crew member, the sound engineer at her movable table weighted down with mystifying devices, perky Francine standing behind her, a black, muscular microphone ("boom") operator holding his boom in the air, headphones on, ready to record, the second assistant waved them into a room which held the director, the cinematographer, two cameras and two camera operators, many lights on stands and, of course, Amanda, looking in a mirror held up by a makeup assistant, an ominous operating table, a tray of scary-looking shiny surgical tools, a prop man squeezed in a corner, a producer with a cup of water, waiting (obviously) to watch Amanda.

Yet there was room enough to perform the scene -- the nurse struggling with the boy who didn't want to get on the operating table, Tad entering because of the boy's yelling, his questioning of the nurse who abruptly tells Tad to get out, Tad not liking it, she insisting, he saying "Let's bring in your supervisor," the boy escaping, the nurse zapping Tad with her electrical prod, Tad falling to the floor (covered at that spot with furniture pads to protect him). This they rehearsed several times after the director explained the "blocking" (positioning of characters physically) and saw Tad's fall to the floor. It was photographed once, by two cameras, simultaneously, from two angles. They (the boy and Tad) got out of position once or twice, which the operator of one camera complained about none too pleasantly, the director asked Amanda would she act more "sinister," and the scene was shot again. The director didn't seem satisfied, and held a consultation with the producer, after which the director spoke with Amanda and then approached Tad.

"We've got an idea here, we think this will be better. She's wearing a tear-away blouse, we thought this might be, uh, one way to go with it. If you are struggling with her, you know, if she tries to push you out, you kind of grab at her and can you yank at the blouse and, uh, tear it a little? What do you think? I can show you." Without waiting for an answer (as if he needed one), he went to Amanda to demonstrate the action, fake-struggling with her, grabbing the open part of her blouse, pretending to pull it away.

"See, here, Tad, it will rip open some. It will be more exciting. Dramatic, okay? Want to try it? Not actually tearing it yet. We only have two blouses rigged to pull out, okay? Try it, will you?"

He stepped back; everyone stepped back except Amanda and Tad. And waited. The producer stuck his head over his shoulder. Tad approached Amanda, thinking she must be embarrassed; they put their hands on each other, but the director said: "Wait. Hold it. Just start by pushing at him, Amanda, and you, Tad, you can resist by grabbing at her arms, okay? Action."

She pushed at Tad, saying "Leave!" and Tad resisted, grabbed her arms, fought a little with her, grabbed at the lapel of her low-cut blouse, faked pulling at it as if it was part of the struggle, and then turned to the director. "That it?" he asked.

"Sure. That's it. Only you could look more angry, Amanda, okay?" He turned to the producer, who nodded his head, then turned to Tad, asking, "Need another rehearsal or do you want to try it?"

"Let's try it," Tad said, stepping back. "You okay with it?" he asked Amanda.

"I guess, only how much will it pull out, you know?" She gestured rather comically toward her breasts, "Like..?"

"Not very much. Don't pull too much, Tad," the director interposed. "Okay, quiet, everyone. Let's shoot one." The assistant yelled "Quiet! Roll sound! Roll camera one. Roll camera two." After receiving confirmation from the sound engineer and the camera operators, he waited for the director to say: "Action," but he didn't, instead he asked: "Can you start a few lines back, Amanda? Tad? What's your line, Tad?"

"Uh, uh, 'Don't do that. Why are you treating him like that?'"

"No," the director said, "after that, after the kid runs out." Shaun was then excused by the assistant director. He went out the door.

Tad said, "Okay. What about my line: 'Let's bring in your supervisor right now?'"

"Good. Good. That'll do. Okay, let's try it. Still rolling?"

"Still rolling," the assistant replied, looking at the cameras. "Sound still rolling?" he yelled out the door.

"Sound rolling," the engineer yelled.

"Quiet!" the assistant yelled.

"Okay," the director said: "Action."

Tad stepped up to an enraged Amanda: "Let's bring in your supervisor right now!"

"Let's you just get out of here, now!"

"I'm not leaving. I want --!" Tad stood his ground but Amanda pushed him so hard he stopped saying his line, which he completed after grabbing her arms: "-- an explanation for this."

Amanda pulled away and pushed at him again, and Tad grabbed one shoulder with one hand, then grabbed the fabric of her collar, pulled, and it ripped open, revealing her bra and breast, slightly, whereupon she clutched the material immediately into place.

"Cut! Cut! Uh, okay, good... but, Tad, I didn't mean to confuse you. Pull, uh, pull harder, pull more clothes away. Okay? Bring in --," but the wardrobe assistant was there already, doing up the blouse, replacing the hidden clips, fixing the collar, checking her work.

"Is that one okay for another take?" the director asked her.

"Yes, sir, I think so, sir." She stepped away. Amanda looked down at herself. It was very quiet on the set. Tad held his tongue from asking her if she was alright.

The director gave a nervous laugh and asked her himself: "Alright, Amanda?"

She laughed too: "Yes."

"Okay. Let's try it again. Pull harder, Tad."

"Sure, okay, I will. I just -- sure." He very nearly asked if they wanted her breasts to be exposed, nipples and all, but couldn't say the words. Anyway, he thought, that must be what they want. Who wouldn't? He also wanted to ask if the bra was 'tear-away,' but didn't.

Then sound and cameras were rolling, the director said: "Action," Tad approached her with his line, she seemed more angry than ever, they gave their dialogue, they pushed and pulled and <u>rip</u> came off the front of the blouse <u>and</u> the low-cut bra from both breasts as they popped out suddenly, and Amanda, in the spirit of things, didn't clutch herself, just looked at Tad in shock, looked at herself, and <u>then</u> covered up.

"Cut! Cut! Great!"

There was one more take, with a new blouse and bra, after which they refilmed the zapping with the electric device (to provide for the torn blouse now being in the scene, at that point), and Tad was finished with his part for the day.

He had one more short scene with Amanda, filmed the next afternoon. But first, in the morning, Tad had an encounter with an escaped "patient" who alerted the waiting room crowd "horrible" things were occurring in the hospital. The listeners were alarmed and went to see what was up. Several were overpowered by guards -- but Tad escaped upstairs, madly looking for his "wife." The audience will know she hasn't been "implanted" with robot circuitry, yet, but he doesn't know either way, giving Tad the opportunity to act and run desperately into two empty rooms when he then hears the kid screaming from another room, in Amanda's clutches. Unable to open the door, he pounds on it, and Amanda appears, assuring him "all is well, not to worry." That was a "cut," because the part of forcing himself inside, precipitating the confrontation and zapping, had already been filmed. Also, from the corridor, they filmed his crawling out the door after being zapped, yelling "Look out!" and collapsing, dead, in the hallway. He looked for Amanda after that, to speak with her, but was told she had left for the day. So he waited in the dressing room, to finish his last scene (actually the <u>first</u> one, for his character, in the movie), a long shot of him entering the emergency room with his limping "wife."

The sound engineer (Dolores, he'd learned) knocked on his door. She had the address and phone number of the theatre where her niece was performing *THE TEMPEST*.

"She's very much hoping you will attend," Dolores said, handing him a note.

"I know. I will. I'm looking forward to it. Thank you," he said, taking the paper.

"She's nice, isn't she?"

"Very nice."

"That's her number there," Dolores said, pointing to it in his hand. "Please call her. Let her know when you're going. Maybe you can get together after the show."

"Fine. But... how old is she?"

Dolores smiled. "Come on, Tad. Don't ask that. And don't ask my age, either!" She laughed and moved down the steps, backwards. "She'll tell you if she wants to, but I won't. And I'll never tell you mine!"

"Thirty, right?"

"Very funny." She walked away but began running to the hospital entrance when the production assistant yelled

"Quiet," and she disappeared into the entrance as he yelled "Roll sound!" After watching, in surprise, Tad looked at the note. Francine had written "Do come, see a fellow Thespian" at the bottom, with hugs and kisses symbols.

"Wow," Tad whispered. The assistant yelled "Rolling!" and "Action." Gunfire issued from the hospital. A crew member outside pretended he was wounded and fell to the ground groaning. The production assistant said "Shhh!" The thin female crew member laughed, provoking another "Shhh!" from the assistant.

His finances were okay -- manageable -- though the horror movie didn't raise him out of credit card debt, but did mean a few months of rent were covered. Sam and he split the thousand dollar rent, plus electric bill, so only food, gas, and cable expenses were left. Four months if he stretched it. He needed that time to get another job. Time to find a more artistic role, a role that would say something about life, about people, about inner reality (viewpoints) as opposed to outer reality (viewed circumstances). He'd seen some like that -- *MILLION DOLLAR BABY*, for instance, and *SHAKESPEARE IN LOVE*. Tad had no hope of landing a part in any movie of that caliber, but he

felt confident there were others out there -- not as good,
but still artistic. Transformational. Touching the
audience rather than merely slamming it around with
violence and crude humor. Although he did enjoy Jackie
Chan movies -- the fighting and the humor were presented in
carefully non-offensive ways, at least for his tastes.
Refinement didn't always equal art, and art didn't always
exclude entertainment. His high school drama teacher felt
that way, and Tad was disposed to agree. The drama
professor at college held "theatre" to an even higher
standard, teaching "low" humor, even in classic works, was
off track. But Tad personally drew the artistic line a bit
lower, as long as a message of value found expression in
the overall content. Sure, *SOME LIKE IT HOT* showed men
pretending to be women (low humor), but finally they eluded
the bad guys and love won over deceit (valuable message).

Not that Tad ever expected to be in such a good movie.
Or was that just his faithless mother talking? Paul Newman
was in excellent movies, and Kirk Douglas. Couldn't Tad
Walsh achieve that much, reach that high, scale such
heights? Didn't the campus paper review say he had a lot
of promise, in addition to "strong blue eyes"? Didn't Zack

push him to try, hadn't his professor cast him in the lead in *U.S.A.*, wasn't Sara on his side?

He saw *THE TEMPEST* at the Redlands Playhouse, the final night. Francine was cute, and recited her lines well. Very impressive, actually, considering it was Shakespeare. Smart girl, advanced for her age. There was a little party backstage she'd told him about, so he waited by prearrangement in the parking lot for her to come out. It took a while -- at least an hour. Tad felt bizarre sitting in his car, but resisted the powerful impulse to split, to forget the whole thing. Yet... he liked her, he was attracted to her energy, her strength, her talent.

Finally Francine exited the rear of the theatre, hugging cast members and others Tad didn't recognize, looked for him, smiled, ran toward him, kissed him on the cheek when he got out to meet her, jumped into the passenger seat, asking, "Did you like it? Did I do okay?"

He nodded, saying, "Yes, of course," got in, drove out of the parking lot fast when he saw the others watching them, and remarked, "You were fantastic, really. Really got a hold of the role."

She reached for his genitals, squeezing them, shocking him, saying, "This is the roll I want to get a hold of!"

"Have you been drinking?" he asked.

"Just a glass of wine."

"Or two."

"Okay, two. It's our last night, after all."

"I'm not saying anything." She let go of him, feeling embarrassed. "I'm so happy, and sad. I can't explain it."

"You don't have to. I know exactly how it feels to finish a play. It's painful."

"It is! Sorry I did that."

"No, really, no, that's good. I didn't mind."

She grabbed him again. "You didn't?"

They parked halfway to her home and made out. She wanted to kiss and kiss. Tad enjoyed it, but she pushed him away and said: "Look. Listen, Tad. I can't do more than this for a while. Do you know what I mean?"

He nodded, not actually knowing what she meant: "It's up to you."

"Because I have to know someone really well. Before anything."

"I get you."

"Thanks." She kissed him, putting her hand on his genitals, rubbing them. Then she stopped. "I should get home. My mother is waiting up. Okay?"

Not feeling sleepy, Tad drove across town, had coffee at the counter at Denny's (one of the few counters left in the entire city), contemplated Francine, strained to understand why her mother had looked so harshly at him when they met, in Francine's doorway. She'd been polite, but little else. Tad perhaps had overdone the friendliness. Was he too old for her daughter? He was only twenty-one, only just. Anyway, it was a cold look, and Tad worried about it. It was like the look his mother had given him many times. Disapproving, but covertly. Hiding something.

He drove in a wide circle, finally parking outside the bungalow complex, going into his house quietly (Sam was no doubt sleeping), poured a short brandy, sat thinking in the dark living room, remembering the great kissing, the warm body against him, the damp hair. Had she washed it after the performance? He thought of her on stage, too, confident, strong, maybe too strong for the character. It amused him she'd recited lines he often couldn't understand, couldn't keep up with, which she had obviously no trouble understanding. Shakespeare was like that. Hard to follow, even when you've read the play beforehand (which he had). Was she smarter than him? That amused him too. Tad eagerly looked forward to seeing her again, to kissing her again, even if she wasn't going to let him do "anything." Until she got to know him "really well."

He did see her again, although it was a very strange date. The mother was friendlier this time, when he picked Francine up. They went to the Westwood V.A. Hospital where her father was, a wounded Desert Storm soldier. One of the very few wounded in that operation (unlike the second attack on Iraq). He was not quite all there, mentally, but Tad didn't dare ask about the extent of his injuries. They stood by his bed for fifteen minutes; Francine began to cry toward the end of the visit. Her father looked at her, feeling her pain, mumbling. "Honey, honey, don't."

Tad shook his hand a second time, thanked him for his service a second time, told him they'd return soon, told him he'd bring him a copy of his horror movie as quickly as possible, patted him on the shoulder, tried not to but did glance at the other bed-ridden heroes, some with visitors, some not, as he and Francine left, two people able to walk

out of the ward, two people who could go on with their
lives outside, who could choose which place to go next,
which activity, which future path, which job, which day to
return for a brief visit, which political candidate to vote
for (well, not Francine, she'd have to wait a couple of
years). But, he thought grimly, those men (and women) can
vote, at least.

Their date continued with another encounter, this time
at Dolores the sound engineer's condo, in Beverly Hills.
Over tea and soft drinks they talked of the play, Dolores's
ex, movies, and life. She called her Fanny, of course, and
served up a snack, and let them into her bedroom for a
make-out session, a surprise to Tad but not to Francine.

In the car she said, exuberantly: "My aunt is the
greatest, don't you think?"

"She's terrific. When can we visit her again?"

Francine laughed. "Oh, like, tomorrow if you want
to."

"No, not that soon. She'd be -- she won't go for
that."

"Sure she would. I'm telling you, my aunt's the
greatest!"

"Well, yes, yeah, I know. But let's wait. Maybe next week. Okay?"

"Okay." She looked out her window. "I can make you come next time, if you want." When he didn't, couldn't, answer, she added: "At least I want to see it, you know what I mean? Okay?"

"See it. Yes, yeah, I know what you mean."

Tad was a little sorry he'd asked her her age, but that was that. If he had sex with her he'd be risking charges, of course. In some states, he knew, from watching the news, sixteen was the age of consent -- like Massachusetts. But not California. California said a woman can't make up her own mind about sex until she's eighteen. Of course, she can get an abortion if she wants without parental notification, or consent. Weird.

Anyway, Tad didn't want to go to jail. But Francine had experience -- she said. Didn't that make a difference? Apparently not. Dolores was for it, but the law wasn't interested in her approval.

On their next date (walking along Hollywood Boulevard and eating lunch at "Fred's Place" near the Chinese Theatre, Francine told him she'd danced naked at parties,

and even traded bedmates one night for fun, with a friend
of hers. They'd all four been in the same bed, doing it
side by side, so the guys just switched girls. Tad had
never heard of such a thing, but she said it wasn't
uncommon with her crowd.

"How often have you done <u>that</u>?" he asked her, at their
table at Fred's.

"Only once. That time. Shocked?"

"No, not shocked," he lied. "Maybe surprised, that's
all."

"I know lots of stuff," she said, smiling that big
smile. "But I've never done anything with another woman."

Another <u>woman</u>, Tad thought. But with a man over
eighteen? Their orders arrived; they ate in silence.
Fred's was crowded -- good food.

"Want to go to Dolores's?" she asked.

"Not today. I'm tired."

"Sure?"

"Yep."

"Come on."

"Francine, I'm twenty-one."

"So? I won't tell anybody, I promise."

"I know."

"Anyway -- I just want to see it," she said. "Hard."

Tad blushed, and Francine laughed.

"I felt it the last time, didn't I?"

"You sure did. <u>Ouch</u>," he exclaimed.

"What?"

"Just kidding." She hit his arm.

Francine ate French fries like a fiend, and after lunch wanted to play pinball at the bowling alley. That lasted about an hour, Tad watching, and playing twice, at her request. He wasn't very good at it.

"Need practice," he said as she jumped again into action, banging the machine over and over with her little hands, to assist her play, scoring huge numbers, getting free plays, laughing and screaming.

He dropped her off in front of her house, in the car kissing her for a long minute, fearing the mother was watching from inside. When he glanced one time at the house Francine said: "Relax! She's at work!" and threw her arms around him, to resume.

Back in his apartment Tad told Sam: "Wow, this girl is so... excited. Not like Sara. Sara was cool, like a cucumber."

"Tell me all about it, man," Sam replied. "Let me get you a beer first." He headed for the kitchen, leaving Tad, in his favorite broken-down easy chair, alone with his thoughts for twenty seconds.

"No, no. I can't tell you any more, now," Tad announced when Sam handed him the bottle. "Please. Thank you."

"Punk." Sam sat down, disgusted, on the couch. "When you win a piece, you had better tell me."

"Okay, I will." He drank gratefully.

"Right-on you will."

"Yeah. But she may not go for it. She said she went with her last boyfriend six months before they did it. I'm not joking."

Sam shook his head in disbelief. "Not true. She's lying."

"I think it's true. Remember, she's only sixteen."

"So? That's nothing these days. My sister was at it at fourteen."

Tad drank, not caring to respond to that family revelation. Then he asked, "So when did you start?"

"Fifteen, I think."

"You don't know?" Tad laughed.

"I know, punk. I was fifteen. My neighbor. And I'm telling you it's a damn bad idea to be involved with a neighbor. Can't escape them when the romance is over!"

Tad, leaving the bungalow compound in the morning, felt as he often did the impulse to buy a hose to water the pathetic grass and scraggly bushes around the front of his apartment, but forgot about it within ten minutes. Sam was auditioning for a fireman movie, just as he had a few days earlier. He hoped Sam would get the part; Tad felt less optimistic about his own chances after seeing the roomful of young men, like himself, who were up for the two white rookie firemen parts. He'd read a lot of the script over at his agent's, and saw that the three parts for black actors offered greater hope for Sam. Still, you never know what the producers would decide. It was a mystery. They never really told you what they were looking for -- maybe they didn't know themselves. "Lightness," "dark qualities," "energy," muscles, innocence, good looks, steadfastness, coolness, what? Like the western series part Tad had tried out for, and not gotten. Seems they wanted a Kevin Costner type. Tad couldn't play that "quiet intensity." He could play energy, action, shyness, or cowboy simplicity, yeah, but not Costner "contained" intensity. He either turned it loose in the reading, jumping around the room, or held it in, speaking his lines softly, sitting in the chair. Maybe he should practice more.

He ate breakfast at Carrows and then called Francine's number, from his car. In those days talking on a cell phone was allowed while driving. She answered breathlessly.

"Awake?"

"I'm up," she responded. "What are you doing?"

"Oh, driving around, waiting to hear from my agent. What's happening?"

"Nothing. My mother's at work. I'm all alone."

"Aren't you supposed to be in school?"

"I dropped out. Didn't I tell you that?"

"Maybe," he said, wondering at that. "Did you?"

"I'll go back. Don't push me."

"What did I say? I'm not pushing you."

"I don't like school, alright? Tests and everything. It's boring. I want to act."

"Right. But, dear, the more you learn the better an actress you'll be."

"You dropped out of college."

"No, I finished two years. I just stopped for a while to see if I could make it in Hollywood. That's not the same thing. But it's your decision."

"I'm going to be in the next production."

"At the playhouse? Good. What is it?"

"Don't know yet."

"You don't know? How can you think you'll be in it, then?"

"They asked me," she said defiantly. "The director of *THE TEMPEST* asked me if I was available!"

"Okay." He didn't want to argue. "You should try to find out what play it is, though. And get a copy of it. The more prepared you are the better."

"I know. Can you come and get me?

"Well, yeah. Now?"

"If you're not afraid."

"What?"

"Of me," she said quietly.

"Ha! What do you want to do?"

"Anything. Just get me the heck out of here. I had to vacuum and do the dishes and I don't want to hang around."

"Okay. I'll be over pretty soon."

"Great. Let's go to Magic Mountain!"

A theme park with a famous roller coaster ride outside of town. "No, let's not," he responded.

"Can't afford it?"

"No, not that, I don't like those rides."

"Wimp."

"I'll pick you up. I have to hang up and call my agent."

"Tell him 'hi' for me."

"Are you serious? I don't --"

"No, you know I'm not serious."

"Okay. 'Bye."

"'Bye."

His agent didn't know anything yet about the fireman's role, but did have another horror movie by the same people as before, coming up soon. Tad didn't feel inclined to do another one, but Franklin said: "More money this time. I can get you three thousand, I bet you."

"Really?"

"Really. I've already put in the call. They think you're good. They're happy with your performance in *MAD SCIENTIST*."

"When's it coming out?"

"*MAD SCIENTIST*? I'll try to get that information. So the new one sounds good?"

"How can I answer that? I haven't read it. What is it?"

"Come by and take a look at the breakdown. I'm having a script sent over. I submitted Destiny for it. Do you know Destiny?"

"Never met her. Is she over there?"

"No, but you ought to meet her. Sweet girl. I prefer my clients to know each other, then when I submit one, I can potentially match others up with them, depending on the parts. Packaging."

"Yeah, packaging. Okay, I'll be over."

"See you."

"Right. Thanks."

"See you," Franklin said.

"'Bye."

Francine ran out the door, purse in hand, wearing white pants, tennis shoes, light blue top with no bra, blonde hair flying, too much blue eye shadow, fairly panting as she jumped in the car.

"Hello!"

"Hi, babe," he said. "Want to meet my agent?"

"Yeah! Now?"

"Now. He said come over."

"Am I dressed okay?"

"Sure you are." He kissed her quickly, shifted into drive, pulled out onto the street, and wondered what Franklin would think of her. He'd have to say she was eighteen.

"I'm going to say you're eighteen. Okay?"

"Fine." She adjusted her blue blouse. "This matches my eye shadow, doesn't it?"

"It does. You look good. Real good."

"Thanks. Are we going now?"

"Um-huh."

"Do I need to audition?"

"Hey, I'm only going there to look at a breakdown. I'm taking you in with me."

"Doesn't he want to see me specifically?"

"That's not what I said, Francine."

"Oh, I thought you did."

The meeting was successful. She acted cute and lively, Franklin stared at her blue blouse, asked questions about her experience (acting-wise), and Tad read the brief summary of the new horror movie, feeling it was trash, not art, but asked Franklin how he could get three thou for him.

"It's two weeks' work. Scale is almost that much, anyway, so I'll push for a little more. I'm confident you'll get it."

"This sounds dumb, like every other dumb movie that's out now. Is this the role?" He pointed to the list on the breakdown, to the part described as "featured role, Spencer." He read it out loud: "A lightning quick wit, a propensity for aggravated assault, joins lead (Mark) in kidnapping infants, dies in climactic farmhouse fire. Names only."

"Well?"

"What's 'aggravated assault,' exactly?"

"I'm not sure," Franklin replied calmly. "Wait until you read the script. That should explain it."

"And what's this: 'names only'?"

"They want names, known actors. But don't worry. I told you they like you from *MAD SCIENTIST*."

"Oh, shit."

Francine laughed, Franklin groaned and said: "Wait until you read it."

"What about Mark, what about that part?"

"Star names only. Look." He pointed to the breakdown. Tad hissed:

"'Star names.' What star will do this?" He read to Francine: "Exciting tale of horror, baby kidnapping, corrupt police, deadly pursuit action sequences, slasher style rampage, main lead's romance fails when Betsy turns Mark over to corrupt sheriff. Violence. Brief nudity. Rough language." Tad shook his head. "Baby kidnapping? Rough language? This is shit."

"Destiny may play one of the young mothers. She likes it. Loosen up, man. Look at the script." He then turned to Francine. "Are you seeking representation, or only planning on stage work?"

"I -- sure. No, not only stage work." She glanced at Tad. "I don't know."

Tad helped her: "She's good, believe me. If you'd like her to read, we can do that. Arrange that."

"I would. Come in anytime. Just call first." He stood up, rather irritated at Tad's display of disdain for the role. "Paula will let you know when the script arrives, if you haven't already talked yourself out of it."

"No, Franklin, I'll read it. Relax."

Francine and Tad stood, Franklin returned to his chair behind the desk, smiling pleasantly, hiding his irritation. He had other idealistic clients. Nothing new to him. But he was a practical man. Money made the world go 'round, not critically acclaimed box office failures.

Francine was happy, when they left, full of secret enthusiasm, propelled by her dreams of success, of a movie career (by procuring Tad's help), just as her aunt had advised. She was on her way now, providing she got the agent's audition, and the contract. Francine knew she had talent -- those other teenage stars had <u>nada</u> on her.

"Come on, come on, do the movie!"

"I have to get it first."

"You will." She kissed his cheek, putting her arm around him, as they drove, and planned her future, thinking it depended on him.

"It's a bullshit movie. Slasher movie."

"Tad! What do you care?"

He didn't answer. How could he explain the feeling, his attraction to art?

"What's wrong?" she asked, finally, staring at him.

"I want to do something better, something with substance. Like _CASABLANCA_."

"What's that?"

Again he didn't answer.

"Whatever it is, you can do more movies later. Get your foot in the door first."

"I'm not going to play a baby kidnapper who probably kills people all through the whole movie."

"Oh, Tad, you don't know that. Anyway, didn't Johnny Depp kill people in _PIRATES_?"

"I suppose so, but that isn't what I'm talking about." He was getting angry, and Francine felt the need to calm him.

"Okay, don't stress out. Let's go to Dolores's. Forget about it."

"No." But he looked at her and said, "Oh, why not?"

So, they did. Her aunt stayed in the living room watching TV. In the bedroom Francine took her clothes off and undressed Tad piece by piece. He slowly fell into the spirit of things; they rolled on the bed; Francine ran out to get a condom from Dolores; they made love.

It was special, it was exciting, he had to admit. Of course, afterward, Tad felt worried, and swore he wouldn't repeat it, and sweated the danger of Francine telling her mother. Little chance of that. She couldn't have told her about those wild parties, could she?

Also he was afraid to tell Sam, so he didn't. The less people who knew, the less chance of the police finding out. But it had been a delicious experience, no question. Only, what? Was he stupid, or what?

He picked up the script later that afternoon, flipped through it, but turned down the chance, arguing with Franklin on the phone, trying to articulate his position, finally conceding the "threshold" could be lower in the future, or, rather, the choices "widened," as Franklin expressed it, felt great relief after hanging up, changed pants, ran at the local track, picked up burgers at Carl's Jr. for Sam and himself, got Pacifico at a 7-Eleven, showered, watched the news, called Francine, spoke lovingly to her, drank a beer until Sam arrive -- elated due to his "rockin'" audition -- and told Sam he'd rejected the horror movie part, that maybe they'd go for a black guy, that Sam should ask Franklin. He didn't say a word about Francine, drank only three beers (not much considering how troubled he felt), complained of being tired, and went to bed.

As it turned out, ironically, he <u>wanted</u> to do the next part, in a Fox Network comedy, with possible future episodes (a 'recurring' role), but they said no the following day. Didn't think he was funny enough in his reading.

Then he lost out on a space alien movie. A good role, too. And the way the invaded town pulled together to resist the aliens, dropping their previous prejudices for the greater common good, felt like "art" to Tad. But he wasn't "right" for the young bank manager role, and in fact they hired an older actor. It wasn't Tad's fault, his agent said -- the part was written wrong, whatever that meant.

His life was wrong, too -- having a relationship with a minor. So what she looked older, knew a lot about life, made her own decisions? The law was the law. He had to get out.

First he helped her with her audition for Franklin. Actually it went very well; Franklin liked her, but said she ought to take more acting classes and come back in a year. It saved Tad the unwelcome task of coming clean about her age -- a fact that couldn't be hidden from the guild and prospective employers.

Francine cried when she heard the news, relayed by Tad, of the decision. But she bounced back, even agreeing with Franklin's assessment. She'd tried. All that was left now, for Tad, was the supremely disagreeable 'break-up' conversation.

As for Francine, she was unsure whether to keep trying to use Tad for her acting career, or to return to high school, or, since she truly did feel something, continue dating him. Definitely Tad was an improvement over her last boyfriend, who'd cheated, who'd made her give handjobs without reciprocal favors, let alone much intercourse. Dolores had said leave him (the old boyfriend), which she had, "sort of," only seeing him off and on to get cocaine (promising him money if she ever got on television). And Tad was certainly an improvement over the wretched former former boyfriend who called too much, begging her to come back. He was older than Tad. Her mother offered some help, telling her to return to school; her father of course couldn't be counted on for advice, in his condition. She'd have to decide all on her own. That's how she'd lived for years, refusing to follow her parents' loose guidelines. But what to do about Tad? Dolores liked him, advising a continuation of the status quo.

He solved her problem for her, taking her to play pinball, and then to a restaurant, fumbling around like most men did, telling her things were risky for him, that he of course cared for her (clear to Francine already), that he was trying to "break it to her gently," he said.

"What's that?" It hurt her unexpectedly.

"You and me, we --"

"What about us?"

"You and me, you know. I like you very much. Could be I love you, except you're sixteen. It's not smart to have a sexual relationship. That's obvious."

"And?"

"And we oughtn't to, that's what."

"If I was older, it would be okay?"

"Of course. And there's that, Francine, when you <u>are</u> older, we can get together, we --"

"Will you still be interested in me?"

Tad grabbed her hand, nearly spilling his coffee. "Absolutely. Are you crazy?"

She didn't cry; she resisted the temptation. "Why don't you call me Fanny?"

"What?"

"Call me Fanny."

He laughed, squeezing her hand. "Really?"

"Don't <u>dare</u> forget!"

"Which? Calling you Fanny or taking up with you again in two years?"

She laughed softly. "Taking up with me." She paused, thinking of something which drew her eyebrows low and her lips tight. "But if you're a big star you'll forget about me."

"I'll not likely be a big star that soon, or ever, and I won't forget about you, at any rate, no matter what happens."

Finally some tears filled her eyes. "You will. You'll find another girl."

"I won't, probably. But... let's see what happens. You could find someone. You <u>should</u> find someone. Don't feel bad. We had a good time."

There wasn't any more to say. He paid the check, drove her to her home, kissed her, walked her to the door, shrugged, patted her on the arm, looked for that big smile, waited until it came, kissed her again, turned and walked away. She yelled "Thanks for taking me to your agent!"

"You're welcome," he yelled, at his car, fighting off the impulse to say, 'I'll call you.' But he did say "'Bye, Fanny!"

It was a black mood, and guilt and pain, that beset him like a dreadful ghost the rest of the week, and longer. She felt it too, abstractly and angrily, yet realizing how her heart had managed to subsume her trickery, how her affection had saved them from misfortune, because she'd accepted Tad's decision, and recognized the rightness of it, rather than resist.

The presidential election came and went, the exit polls indicating John Kerry had won but the final total indicating George Bush had. Tad's Republican friend from college, Hal, called, saying people lied outside the polling places, but Tad didn't understand.

"Why?" he asked suspiciously.

"I don't know," Hal responded.

"I mean, you say they were afraid to tell the truth? That people voted for Bush, yet when they came out, said they'd voted for Kerry? Why would they do that?"

Hal got angry. "It's just a theory!"

"Sure, sure." Normally when Hal got angry Tad just let it drop, but he pushed on: "It's a theory. But a theory has a foundation, doesn't it? What is the foundation?"

"I don't know, Tad."

"Yet you believe it?"

"I didn't say I believed it!"

"Where did you hear this, anyway?"

"I don't know, Tad. It doesn't matter."

"Yes it does. Whose theory is this?"

"Okay, it's stupid. Never mind."

"I'm only asking. Sounds like b.s."

"What else could explain the difference?"

"That a rhetorical question? Voting fraud, like last time. The exit polls were right."

"Nobody can fix the results! It's too hard. And you liberals would raise hell."

"First of all, I'm not a liberal. Second, you're being naïve to think the count can't be fixed. They did it the last time, didn't they?"

"Not true," Hal said. "It wasn't proven."

"That depends on which radio show you listen to."

"Oh, right, you listen to that left-wing one -- what is it?"

"Pacifica Radio," Tad replied. "It's better than --"

"So keep listening, I don't care. Don't cry to me if there's another terrorist attack."

"What the hell does that mean?"

"You liberals aren't going to protect the country! You're too weak. I don't even want to talk anymore. Goodbye." He hung up. Tad followed suit, sitting in his old easy chair, frustrated, angry at Hal, angry at his government, angry at himself, angry at the news media, not knowing what the truth was, sorry he couldn't be with "Fanny" anymore, sorry Sam had a job and he didn't.

For two days he brooded, shopped, cooked simple meals for himself and Sam, who came in talking about riding on the fire engine, sliding down the poles, not liking a couple of the cast members, inviting Tad to the set, having a female friend over to spend the night, winking at Tad.

Somehow he had to get Amanda's number. He should have asked her for it when they were working; now, weeks later, there was no chance. Asking Dolores was definitely out. She wouldn't have it anyway. And he didn't want to ask the director. Or the producer. He thought and thought. Going to the hospital might succeed. She worked there. He might be able to find her. Then he hit on it: the film's production office would have everyone's number. And he just might lie his way into obtaining Amanda's. Thinking up a good story was crucial.

It took half a day, but an idea came to him. First he thought of saying they'd talked about his agent, but probably everyone tried that. So he called saying he had a script for her to read, that she'd been interested in it, that there was a role for her, that he'd forgotten to get her phone number. It worked. The secretary knew him, anyway, from the movie, and she even offered to give him Amanda's address. He took it. Then he realized there was little need to lie at all, most likely, and feel bad. He didn't believe in lying. It's a sin. And his mother did so much of it, he loathed it.

He stressed out for another day, reluctant to call Amanda, but wanting to. He visited Sam's film set, a downtown firehouse, watched Sam eat lunch in one scene and stack hoses in another. Boring.

Tad called her, but without any substantial hope Amanda would go on a date, assuming (correctly, as it turned out) she'd have a boyfriend. Jealous, too, considering her great body, so she'd sweetly decline any invitation. Yet, one must try.

After preliminaries, he fast-forwarded to the chase: "Say, uh, do you have days off from work?"

"Yeah, but, don't tell me you want to go out?"

"Kind of, yes. But -- is that so bad?"

"No, no, I just thought you were asking me, that's all. Don't be insulted. But, it's only my boyfriend wouldn't like it."

"Okay. Serious?"

"Yeah. Sorry. Thanks for asking."

"Must be normal, for you."

"Think so? Not actually."

"Come on," Tad said, "everyone, anyone would want to go out with you."

"Why?"

"Because of..." he began, then halted, then boldly pressed on: "You have those two beautiful, attractive, big..."

"Yes?"

"Eyes."

"Wow," she laughed loudly. "You're in trouble now."

"Really? Funny, I thought that would keep me out of trouble!"

"Well, I'm bashful about my body, that's what, and I don't like -- you can imagine -- the constant references... all my life, since... high school, at least; before, even."

"References to your eyes?" He chuckled. "I'm kidding. I sympathize with you. I was being clever, there, I admit, but, Amanda, don't you know how lovely your eyes are? Seriously."

"Well, maybe, but they aren't the main conversational point, usually." She giggled.

"Now who's making hidden references to... you-know-what?"

"What?"

"Hey, I saw them, remember?"

"Yeah. And thanks to you now the whole world will."

"I was told to pull that hard."

"Did you have to?" She giggled again.

"Of course. You want me to, uh, reject the director's order? And the producer's?"

"That slimeball. They told me it was his idea. The wardrobe was rigged before I even came in. Mary Lou had to prepare it the night before. She told me."

"Didn't anybody ask you about it?"

"Yeah, right. The director, Mike, he did, that day, before I worked. Said he didn't like it, but the producer did."

"Oh, sure."

"Can we change the subject? I haven't even told my boyfriend. He'll go ballistic."

"Really?" Tad braved another question: "You didn't mind so much, did you? After all, you must know how wonderful your breasts are."

She didn't answer for a moment. Had he gone too far? "No, I don't, frankly."

"They are."

"You think so?"

"Come on, really, Amanda. Are you kidding me?"

"Sort of. You're sweet, you know that?"

"Thanks."

"I'd go out with you if it wasn't for --"

"You would?"

"Uh-huh," she said.

"I'm really happy to hear that. Honestly. I'd thought we could go to this restaurant in Malibu -- at Paradise Cove -- and get a table by the window that looks out at the beach."

"Great. But I can't."

"I know. I'm just telling you. And I'd only look at your eyes the whole time." He chuckled to let her know he was being humorous, but he didn't have to. She laughed more loudly than ever, to his great relief, and said:

"You're funny. My boyfriend has no sense of humor. He even hates my co-workers, who are gay, I tell him, but he doesn't believe me."

"Amanda, maybe you shouldn't be telling me these things about him."

"Why not? Why shouldn't I?"

"Because, I'm attracted to you, and I want to tell you to leave him. That's bad."

"Oh, I get it. You're attracted to me?"

"Are you teasing me? Sure."

"I'm not teasing you, no. Asking you. Maybe I like hearing it. Maybe I don't get asked out all the time like you think. Maybe what I get are offensive pick-up lines, and nasty remarks. Never mind."

"Wow. Sorry. I mean, I'm sorry you talk like that. I mean, how people can be so sleazy. But, sure, I'm attracted to you. You think I'm not serious about your eyes? And your... courage? I saw you on the set, remember?"

She laughed. "Here we go again."

"No, please, I'm sounding full of it, but I'm not. You were brave on the set. And especially since you're not really an actress. I mean, not trained. You know."

"Thanks, Tad. I believe that's sincere."

"It is. Anyway, uh, watch out for your jealous boyfriend, okay? And --"

"It's not only him. My stepfather is that way too. It sucks."

"Wow. Sorry. Can't you keep away from him?"

"No. He's in the house right now, so I can't say any more. I guess you shouldn't call, either."

That pushed him back. "I understand. Take care of yourself. You've got my number there? In your phone?"

"Yes."

"Call anytime you need me -- that sounds corny, but, really -- I'm concerned about you. That's dramatic. Sorry. But... I hope we work together again." Amanda didn't respond, so Tad asked, "Do you have an agent?"

"No."

"Want to go in to meet with mine?"

"Not a good idea," she said.

"Why?"

"Why?"

"Because an acting career isn't exactly being encouraged around there?"

"Uh-huh," she said, quietly.

"Oh. Guess not. Anyway, call if you need anything. I'm not joking."

"Thanks. Can I ask you something?"

"Sure."

She lowered her voice. "Do you have a girlfriend?"

"I do not. Used to. Not now."

"I've got to go, Tad. Thanks for everything."

"'Bye." They both hung up.

Sam finished his fireman's part. Tad got an interview for a role in an episode of a WB sitcom. Nothing came of it. Zack left a message suggesting lunch on Saturday, but Tad didn't return his call. He ran at the track, read part of a Tennessee Williams play, tried to do a few speeches from it, left a message of his own for Mr. Christian, his old drama teacher, suggesting lunch with him and Zack, on Saturday, felt guilty he hadn't invited Sam, even though Sam hadn't been a student of Mr. Christian like he and Zack, checked his bank balance, got tacos for dinner, lay around musing, thinking about Fanny, thinking about Sara, thinking about Amanda.

When Sam came in from a workout at the gym, he invited him to the lunch.

"Saturday?"

"Uh-huh," Tad said.

"Can I bring Jasmine?"

"Well, I need to run it by Zack and Mr. Christian. They won't say no, don't get me wrong. Just a courtesy thing."

"Alright." He lay on the floor, stretching. Tad called Zack first, telling him he'd invited Mr. Christian and Sam and his girlfriend.

"She ain't no girlfriend!" Sam yelled, heading for the bathroom. Nevertheless, Zack agreed, promising to think of a place to go.

When the phone rang later, it was neither Zack nor Mr. Christian, nor even his agent.

"Hello?"

"Tad?" Female voice.

"Yes. It's me."

"Hi. Amanda. Sorry to bother you. Are you busy?"

"Not busy. No bother. Hi, how are you?"

"Not very good. I had a fight, a huge fight, with my stepfather. He's throwing me out of the house."

"You're kidding me."

"He's flipped. Completely. I can't tell you. But, Tad, I called my mom who said she'd let me move in there, but they don't have much room, and I was just wondering, you were so sweet, I can't say it. I can't ask you. But, can I stay with you for a while? You don't have anyone there, you said. I'm so sorry. But --"

"Of course you can," he said quickly, without thinking. "I don't have much room, either, but, of course. Are you alright? Do you need help?"

"No, I'll just bring a few clothes. Thank you! Oh, thank you --"

"I do have a roommate, he's fine, he has his own bedroom. Should I come get you?"

"I have a car, no, thank you, but... do you have a couch?"

"A little one. I'll sleep on it, you take my room. It's okay."

"What? Never!" she exclaimed. "I can sleep on the couch, it doesn't matter. Just for a while. I can pay you."

"Skip that. Let me give you my address."

"Okay, can I call back for it? I want to pack. Are you sure this is alright?"

Was he sure? But... "What about your boyfriend?"

"Didn't I tell you? We broke up for good this time. He's a terrible person. My stepfather and he -- oh, I'll tell you later. Can I call you in a few minutes?"

"Sure. Call me when you're ready."

"Thanks. See you." She hung up.

Tad closed his phone and let his mouth drop open. Sam came out of the bathroom, showered, wearing a long robe, crossed to the kitchen, looking puzzled at Tad's countenance.

"What's the matter with you, buddy?"

She moved in. Sam didn't grouch much after he saw her. He thought it way funny when Tad insisted on taking the sofa. Amanda resisted to the point a compromise was reached -- they'd both sleep in the bed -- it was large enough, queen size.

"Certainly, it's fine like this," Amanda said, unpacking and hanging up her clothes. "The couch is too little even for one person."

Trying to lighten the tension, Tad joked: "As long as you keep your hands off me!"

She giggled, putting underwear in a drawer. "More correctly, if you can keep your hands off me."

"Another thing," he said, moving close to her and lowering his voice. "I didn't tell you my roommate is African-American. That's not a problem, is it?"

"No, no, no. I don't have a problem with that. My ex-boyfriend is black, too." She giggled once more, but said seriously, "He worked at the hospital until they fired him -- for stealing." She sat on the bed beside her open suitcase. "He swore he wasn't guilty, but there was a witness. Dumb. Anyway, that's not why we broke up. Can I buy you guys dinner?"

"Me, you can, if you want to. Sam's going out."

"I'll tell you the whole sad story."

"I'm sweating in anticipation." He was sweating, alright, but not due to that. How could he sleep at night, now?

Mr. Christian called before they left. He politely declined the invitation -- busy on Saturday. It was a long drive, anyway. "Next time we'll go to your neck of the woods," Tad told him.

At dinner Amanda told what _was_ a sad story. Her ex-boyfriend had pulled a gun on her stepfather, they had struggled, the gun went off, firing into the ceiling. Police were summoned. Her ex was arrested, released on bail. Her stepfather flew into a rage, demanded she leave, even though she had broken up with the guy two days earlier.

There was more to the story. A lot more.

Amanda rode horses with her stepfather on the weekends at his ranch east of Los Angeles, and, she admitted, gave him oral sex in a tradeoff. During the week, she said, he wouldn't bother her. She worked at the hospital, cleaning rooms, preparing beds, helping the nurses tend to patients, some of whom she gave massages. But not sex, she assured Tad. The stepfather didn't charge her rent, but did ask her to cook. He had a cleaning lady, yes, but Amanda worked increasingly hard as his demands increased. One night she told her ex about the oral sex; he exploded, mad at them both, called her names, broke up with her on the spot. Abandoned her on a corner. She'd taken a cab. He called to apologize but she wouldn't go back to him. He was mean, anyway, she said, twice slapping her, a year ago, but promising not to do it again. She didn't trust him. After he was fired she <u>really</u> didn't trust him. She was glad to be free, she said, but Tad would be justified having second thoughts, and could throw her out too, if he wanted, but hoped he wouldn't. Of course, he didn't.

That night Amanda was tired, went to bed first, after a shower, wearing long sleeping attire, yet couldn't fall asleep. She was in a depressed, partially shocked state. The gun, the stepfather, the previous breakup. Thank God for Tad, she thought. But he hadn't better make a move on her -- she wasn't feeling anything close to <u>that</u>. Also, a fact she'd concealed from him, her mother had basically

refused to take her in, partly because of past bad feelings

stemming from Amanda's choosing the stepfather over her.

But he had an empty house and a ranch with horses, and her

mother had a new man and a small place. Elsa, a fellow

hospital employee/friend, may have given her a bed to sleep

in, or a small cot, actually, but Amanda chose to ask Tad

first. Sam's presence didn't bother her, except Amanda had

residual fear, now, due to Terrence -- her ex. His temper,

his violent tendencies. Just because he too was black

didn't mean Sam was like that, but she couldn't help

worrying about it. She'd just see how it all worked out.

When Tad came in to go to bed she pretended she was

asleep, and thought most likely he was pretending too

(which he was), but she finally went to sleep out of sheer

exhaustion. He fell asleep more quickly than he'd

predicted, feeling happy she was there.

In the morning it was a bit uncomfortable -- she woke

him up rolling over, hitting his head with her arm,

apologized and sped to the bathroom, saying "Good morning,"

as she closed the door. And locked it. He waited until

she went to the kitchen, wearing a robe, and felt strange

using the bathroom after her, but it was his decision, all this, and he would stick to it if she did.

As it turned out Sam hadn't come in, all night, feeling his own form of discomfort, pressuring his "non-girlfriend" Jasmine to let him stay over. It hadn't taken much pressure, really. But he sure wasn't going to call the bungalow <u>first</u>, before returning. If they were there, they were there. It wasn't a situation of <u>his</u> making, after all.

Amanda said she would get more of her personal things on her way to work, was that okay? Of course. Sure? Of course. She'd get her own place right away. No rush, Tad told her, you're welcome to stay as long as you need to.

What none of them knew was just how angry the stepfather was, feeling betrayed and vengeful toward Terrence and Amanda and now this actor she was moving in with. The pain of betrayal, whether justified or not, sears a mind like a hot poker, driving away reason, burning away logic, destroying any vestige of cold indifference. He'd have his revenge, and he'd have it from whomever stood in his way. However, when she returned to the house he did let her in, let her gather more clothes and papers and toiletries, makeup, photos, bed sheets, but he wasn't about

to ask her back. She'd call him with her new address, she
reluctantly agreed, hoping in her heart she wouldn't have
to, somehow, and thanked him, even, spiritlessly, for
allowing her to stay all these past months (seven). She
even repeated her apology about Terrence's behavior, and
left, secretly mad at what she now saw as this man's
selfish cruelty.

Work was easier than she'd expected, partly due to the
growing attitude of freedom and lightness which her new
circumstance produced.

A week went by full of trepidation, for Tad, and joy,
for Amanda; nights were difficult, both feeling
uncomfortable, and yet curiously peaceful. Tad used mental
discipline to <u>not</u> think of her beside him, Amanda thanked
God for him being beside her, not grabbing at her, or
insisting she comply with his desires, glad he never made
innuendos or sly overtures, but unintentionally it was she
who touched him, in the night, once waking to find her knee
up on his leg, her face against his back, and another night
waking to find her hand scrunched under his chest as Tad
slept face down, inches away. Once when their feet
collided, he sat up to say he was sorry. It was hot under

the blanket, so the third night they slept under sheets, only. By the end of the week she stopped wearing long bottoms, only wore a thin cotton top and baggy shorts. He stayed in his sweat pants and T-shirt, and Amanda was surprised to notice she wished he wasn't wearing that shirt.

The tallest building on Sunset Boulevard contained one of the smallest agencies in Hollywood: Turner Talent, with one agent and one secretary, Paula. Zack had signed as a client right out of high school and worked off-and-on as a teenager on teenage TV shows, earning up to a thousand a gig. Tad signed and didn't score much until Franklin, only twenty-six years old, gave Tad common sense advice:

"Stop behaving like you're a different person than you are. Forget the Montgomery Clift crap. Act like Tad. During the audition you can behave like a different person if it's called for, but not all the time, especially not during the interview."

Tad was in the leather client's chair in Franklin's plain office in the tall building. He looked at his partly bald agent, in coat and tie, behind a desk covered with scripts, mostly unread, a telephone, a box of mail, mostly unopened, and a small laptop. Franklin waited for his response, patiently.

"Well, being myself, you know, how can that get me hired? Seems better to be what they want, be someone who --"

"You don't know what they want. You can't know until you ask questions, and they tell you, and you give the reading. Let them tell you. Don't leap to conclusions. I've been in your position, I know about this. Everybody does it at first, don't feel embarrassed. I would go in there trying to act like Marlon Brando. Me!" He laughed, flexing a bicep, nearly nonexistent, under his jacket sleeve. "Show them you can play a tough guy <u>during</u> the reading, but don't walk in there pretending from the get-go."

"But... what if I don't get the reading? They may pass on me just from the interview, there's a good chance I can --"

"No, Tad. Listen to me. The majority of young actors in this town don't even <u>get</u> interviews, but my father built up this agency, it has prestige. I can ask for interviews, and get them, ordinarily. The point is, if you don't look right they won't let you read, anyway. I'm telling you.

Those days are all but over. No more leisurely getting-to-know you stuff. But pretending to be someone you're not will look false. They won't like it. Just discuss the part, just talk it up, your ideas, your... grasp of the part. But don't act different than you. Okay? Until the actual audition." He smiled like a doctor explaining a disease to a patient, assured he could cure it if the patient would follow his instructions.

After that conversation Tad adjusted his behavior during initial interviews -- but with a twist. Instead of "pretending" to be a character, he "was" the character: he walked in there as if he was himself, acting like himself, what they wanted. As if he didn't have a clue what they wanted, but if the character was, say, a weak brother who hated his successful older brother, Tad established in his mind before going in that that was Tad's situation in real life and felt like it during the meeting, talking to the casting agent or producer as if he, Tad, was weak and did have a brother out there whom he hated, picturing the brother getting all the girls, all the acclaim. Or if the role was as rookie fireman, Tad established in his mind, prior to the meeting, that he could climb ladders and spray fires with hoses and yet still needed experience, was willing to learn, wasn't hardened and cynical. It didn't always work, but it helped. He'd relate stories about whatever fit, like having an older brother, revealing a subtle dislike, or that he'd put out a neighbor's backyard fire once, expressing excitement, describing it. Eventually he accomplished what Zack didn't: getting into feature films. The horror movie had needed a college student, a newlywed fairly innocent type. That's how he thought of himself during the initial interview.

Tad was lucky because he fit that role naturally, merely assuming mentally he'd just married Sara. That was easy. But less-than-natural personas were more difficult to pull off. Of course this wasn't exactly following Franklin's advice, but it was close. The "reading," the audition, doing dialogue from the script, came across better. In a way Franklin was right. To Tad it was method acting -- "living" the part, not just "faking" it. And somewhere between those two forms of behavior, "pretending" and "being," there was a narrow line, vaguely distinguishable, quite similar to Tad's acting nice to a customer at Murray's Fashions when he'd felt tired at the end of a hard day, but yet, he was still Tad. So, behaving nice at work wasn't "fake," exactly, it was true to his personal decision to be pleasant to every customer, even though it required an effort. People on stage play all sorts of ages, or ethnicities, and hopefully are convincing. How? By pretending? Not actually, if, in reality, they keep on believing, as much as possible, they <u>are</u> that character at the time. Franklin knew what he was talking about -- the first meeting needs authenticity, not posturing. Tad simply took it a step further, being himself, yes, but that "himself," through preparation and adjustment, could be the sort of person the part called for.

He tried this method when Franklin sent him out for a part as a 1930's bank robber. Tad thought back to when he'd broken into a house as a kid. That was the "attitude" for the interview: how he'd felt walking through that house, ducking below windows, opening drawers and closets, listening for a car in the driveway. Probably the casting agent thought he was a criminal. Anyway, he auditioned and was officially offered the role. But then came second thoughts about the movie.

It was another patently violent entertainment, void of redeeming qualities aside from the bloody comeuppance the robbers get at the end. Except unfortunately, in Tad's view, the glamorized leader escapes. A murderer, not a hero, presented as a regular guy "forced" to commit crimes, to hurt others, by the Depression-era grip of poverty and insensitive wealthy businessmen. That outcome bothered Tad, even though he wasn't playing the lead.

He complained to Amanda about the project, but she was unsympathetic. In fact, she was thrilled, and told him so.

"What's wrong with you? Tad, Tad, wouldn't this make your future more..." she struggled for a proper word... "you know, brighter? If you do this?"

"Hell no, it doesn't feel like it."

"Or, how about... sweeter?" He was sitting on the couch. She stood before him, the memo from Franklin in her hand.

Tad smirked, shaking his head 'No.'

"Or..." she thought of it... "more hopeful?"

"Not much... but, yeah, some." He bit his fingernail, then pulled it away, and tilted his head up, looking at her beautiful eyes, his resolve dissolving. But he snatched the paper from her grip and tossed it onto the floor. She sat down beside him, his eyes following her. She squinted at him, puzzled, confused.

"You <u>must</u> be happy about it. Aren't you glad? Aren't you going to take it?"

"I will, I suppose. But it ain't much."

"Isn't."

"Isn't."

She picked up the letter, shaking it near his face. "A job, man, a movie part!"

"A <u>little</u> one. A few days. But, sure, it's okay." He bit that fingernail again. She looked at the paper and read aloud:

"I'm sending this deal memo along with a page of revised dialogue. Let me know what you think. Franklin."

Tad leaned his head back, against the top of the couch, staring at the ceiling, moaning, behaving like a child who must clean his room.

In the morning he brushed his teeth and did his usual sit-ups (having read that his hero Paul Newman routinely did sit-ups in the morning) (not that Tad could do as many as Paul Newman purportedly did), ate a toasted English muffin, drank coffee, looked out the window, recalling Amanda's wisdom from the previous night, and regretted his telling her he would take the part. Shooting guns at Feds

and participating in bank holdups wasn't his idea of art.
Playing the lead in *U.S.A.* by John Dos Passos, now <u>that</u> was
"art." The satisfaction he'd felt then, and his scary
decision to enter the acting profession, had been founded
essentially on the premise he would "create" roles, would
be an "artist," would perform in artistic movies, receiving
whatever reward resulted due solely to art, not mere
entertainment -- the difference between, for instance,
BUTCH CASSIDY AND THE SUNDANCE KID (art) and *THE TOWERING
INFERNO* (entertainment). The obvious reality that his hero
Paul Newman appeared in both of those films deterred Tad
not the slightest: those were Newman's choices -- Tad
would stick to art. And make money doing it, like another
one of his heroes, Peter O'Toole.

     But he'd take this job, dumb as it was. Food on the
table. Electricity for the house. Gasoline in the car.
Shoes on his feet, etc. All reasons to take the role. At
ten he left a message for Franklin, who never seemed to get
to his office that early: "Okay, man, it's cool, I'll play
the bank robber, the supporting role of a worthless bank
robber." Breakfast at Carrows followed. A feeling of
remorse dogged him all day. But spending money at the
grocery store reinforced Tad's recognition of financial

needs prompting this artless choice. And phoning Amanda
after hearing his agent's exuberant return message
unburdened Tad of that feeling of remorse -- she was <u>so</u>
pleased, <u>so</u> happy, <u>so</u> excited.

There was dialogue to be learned. And that meant, of
course, much more than simply 'learning' it. The words,
the phrases, the sentences, the speeches must be memorized
in a particular way: with the ability to recall and repeat
them easily at any given later date, whenever the scenes
were scheduled to be filmed. Tad dove into it, learned and
relearned each word, repeating them over and over up to the
first day of shooting. Luckily this bank robber didn't say
very much, and Tad didn't have to repeat long speeches as
are required for, say, Eugene O'Neill plays.

The first day arrived. Cast and crew assembled in a
remote area outside Los Angeles; Tad drove to the location,
was shown his unpretentious yet adequate dressing room,
changed into bank robber circa 30's wardrobe, waited calmly
for his moment. By nine o'clock he was summoned to the set
(an alley behind the "bank," which was really an abandoned
30's style building fixed up with "dressing": fake bank
entrance, the name "Fidelity Security" painted above the

entrance), placed in a '36 Chrysler, given a Tommy gun, told to fire it behind him as the car raced down the alley. His run from the entrance to the waiting car would be filmed later. Tad had to conjure up those feelings consistent with having just run to the car with the stolen loot in a satchel as he and two others made their getaway. They climbed in, "Action" was called, even for a rehearsal, and the car whipped down the alley, straight toward two cameras at the other end. A bank guard was to follow, around the corner, on foot, firing his pistol.

Tad was to, and did, shoot at, but miss, the guard, and the car raced between the cameras. Okay. Some lighting adjustments were made while Tad stood around, sans gun (lifted from him by the prop assistant) and the car was returned to "first position." His fellow criminals joked, waited, pulled at their uncomfortable vintage suits, got last-second makeup touch-ups, were told to return to the getaway car around the corner, climb inside and "get ready." Tad laughed when his seatmate said: "Now I know how Warren Beatty felt!" But it was just a not-too-funny-on-set joke. Better than any Tad could think of, though. *BONNIE AND CLYDE*, he thought. That was artistic. The driver revved the engine. The main robber, in the front seat (the star of the movie), talked on his cell phone until the loud words: "Quiet, everyone!" thundered from the assistant director. Tad was given his Tommy gun through the window. The "bank guard" stood at a distance, staring at Tad's gun, holding his pistol at his side. "Roll sound. Roll cameras one and two!" Such screaming. Like no one can hear? Tad took a breath, conjured up the just-having-robbed-a-bank-and-jumped-into-the-car feeling, lifted his gun to point through the window, waited for "Action!" which the director hollered after a brief interval.

Zoom, the driver drove the car around the corner, Tad leaned more out the window, waited the seconds he'd been instructed to wait, fired a short burst, then another. The car raced down the alley, the bank guard ran into view, firing his pistol, Tad shot another burst which naturally, although only blanks, "missed" the target, the guard flinched and fired again, the car drove past the cameras, the director yelled "Cut!"

After some closer camera work, more gunfiring, more waiting, more feeble joking -- "Hey, I hope these are really blanks!" -- everyone had lunch at tables set up near the 'bank.' Then more makeup, closeups on the star in the passenger seat looking grim and handsome but not appropriately worried his gang could get caught (in Tad's opinion), Tad and the other secondary robbers, along with the weary guard (who was exhausted from repeatedly running around the corner and down the alley firing his pistol), were told they had finished for the day. Tad changed his clothes in his miniscule dressing room, went to the makeup trailer to have some of the makeup removed, initialed the production assistant's paperwork, said goodbye to the others (not the director -- he was busy consulting with the cinematographer [a woman of no mean expertise]), found his car a few blocks away, with a ticket on the windshield, and drove to his house where he washed off the remainder of his makeup and fell onto the couch thinking: well, it wasn't completely inartistic.

There were two more scenes, with dialogue, the next day, for Tad, one of which he enjoyed because it was a heated argument among the thieves concerning future strategy. The lead actor pushed one of the thieves around, Tad yelled in protest, and finally a fateful decision was made to pull one more heist in a nearby town, which turns out bad. But that sequence was to be filmed next week, so

Tad had four days off, including the weekend, until Monday's shooting. He lolled around his apartment/house, talked to Sam about the movie, finished a book (*MADAM BOVARY*, which he didn't like much), took Amanda to a movie (*THE MALTESE FALCON* at the Nuart Theatre). Tad called his mother, getting into an argument.

Sunday night he went to bed early and woke up Monday morning full of excitement and energy. After makeup, on the set, the director told him a stunt double would do his death scene (a fall from a window) but Tad would be allowed to be in the shot where his character takes the first of many G-man bullets. He was fitted with 'squibs,' explosive devices under his clothes, so when he was 'shot' they popped, producing 'blood.' As it turned out he was shot three times and fell back toward the window, dropping his Tommy gun, before the director yelled "Cut!" They did the scene four times, and Tad was weary of it by the last take, noticing the director was more interested in photographing the squibs than his grimacing face. 'Someday,' he thought to himself, 'my face will be more important than fake blood.'

Now that he'd found out where the cast and crew parking was, he didn't get any more tickets. The drive

home was a sorrowful one. For some reason it bothered him
that he'd finished his last scene and wouldn't be in the
movie any further. His mother had criticized the shortness
of his part -- perhaps that was upsetting him. What did
she know? He was happy to be working on a feature film,
and wanted nothing to do with her advice: "Get in a soap
opera."

During the time of Tad's employment the stepfather
Vince left a harassing message on Amanda's cell phone,
ordering her to return to his house, threatening to track
her down and bring her forcibly back. She hadn't given him
her new address, but she wasn't feeling secure simply due
to that -- some way or another he'd find her, she was
convinced. Amanda reported the message to her mother, who,
despite sympathy, said she'd told her so, that Vince was
"trouble."

Would he ruin her arrangement with Tad and Sam?
Probably. She could report it to the police, but held off.
She also feared he would show up at work, or trick the
hospital records office into providing him her new address.

Meanwhile Sam made several sexual comments which
irritated her. How did she know he wouldn't rape her? She

didn't. It's one thing to say a person wouldn't dare, another to believe the person wouldn't. She'd been raped twice as a student at parties where drinking and wildness played a role. She'd reported neither instance, but was forced to have an abortion due to one.

She'd felt ashamed but not guilty. Her self-esteem was just high enough to prevent wicked self-recrimination; the secrets bothered her, nevertheless, and Amanda withdrew emotionally, distorting her relationships with men. Sometimes she considered breast-reduction surgery, other times she flaunted her assets. She threw herself into work -- it gave her a feeling of stability and a good excuse to avoid parties -- parties where further problems could occur.

Terrence had charmed her, at first, then abused her. Now, living with Tad (without romantic entanglement) fit her emotional needs. But the looming threat of her stepfather's acrimony and Terrence's unpredictability frightened her. Nowhere to run. Confiding in her co-workers helped little -- she never told them the entire story.

Often, at night, she wished Tad would hold her, but couldn't bring herself to ask. If only he'd do it on his own!

He, respectful of her space, such as it was, resolutely fought the desire even to touch her, let alone hold her. These thoughts caused restless nights for both of them.

One week after Vince's harassing message she related it to Tad; he deserved to know. He, in turn, told Sam, who responded, "Death to all tyrants! Let him try something!"

Amanda began to get up too early, leave the house too early, arrive at work too early, and was consequently more tired after her shift than usual. When Tad questioned her about it she denied being upset about Vince.

Two weeks, three weeks, four weeks, and Sam landed another part, this time as a cop in a low-budget thriller entitled: *PUT DOWN*. The lunch with Zack had gone well, but for Zack spending the duration speaking of his series, his co-stars, his rosy future if the series was "picked up" for another season. Jasmine hadn't attended. Sam didn't like Zack much -- complaining afterward he talked "all the time, like a hungry rat."

"Well, he paid for the lunch," Tad replied.

"Doesn't entitle him to tell me his life story."

"So you don't want to go the next time?"

"You got that right." He pointed his finger emphatically. They were in the living room. Amanda was at work. The phone rang -- Tad's.

"Excuse me. Hello?"

"It's Kiko. How you doing?"

"Good, what's up? Still robbing banks?"

"No, we finished that weeks ago. But remember you said you would run with me in the morning, sometime?"

"I remember."

"How about tomorrow?"

"Let's do it. What time?"

"Eight?"

"Eight's okay," Tad said. "I'll meet you there."

"Cool. See you then. Everything okay with you?"

"Just waiting for my agent to call," Tad responded.

"Me too, brother. Keep the faith."

"Okay, Kiko. Listen, I have to go. See you tomorrow."

"Cool. Right on. See you tomorrow."

"'Bye." He hung up. Sam was staring at him. "Friend from *TRAPPED*, in the cast. He was the second lead. Nice guy."

"Kiko?"

"Asian," Tad explained.

"An Asian gangster?"

"He looks American."

"Yeah, like I do."

"What?"

"You never see any black old-time gangsters, that's what I mean. Baby Face Amos, you know."

Tad laughed. "Maybe someday. Want to join us? At eight?"

"No," Sam said, standing up from the sofa, flexing his arms. "Want to join me at the gym?"

"No. I don't do weights very well."

"You could use it, skinny boy."

"No, you go ahead, Arnold."

"I'll be baaack."

The alarm clock had awakened Amanda, although she fell asleep after Tad left for his run. Then she woke up, concerned she was alone in the house with Sam, in the next

room. She was afraid of Terrence, not Sam, but
differentiating the two was close to impossible,
emotionally. Maybe she was racist, and never realized it
until this moment. What other conclusion could be drawn?
If Tad's roommate was white, she'd be less afraid. That
was the sad truth. But that wasn't Sam's fault. She'd
have to live with this, or move out. She couldn't discuss
it with Sam. Too insulting for him, too weird for her.

Meanwhile Zack didn't fulfill his lunchtime promise to
find roles for Tad and Sam in an episode of his series.
It's not that he forgot to -- it's that deep inside he
didn't want them even casually taking away from him, on
film. Many actors (and actresses, to a lesser extent) fall
into this abyss of selfishness without reasonable cause.
No one is going to take away from them by playing other
parts -- it's a false fear, an invalid supposition, but one
that keeps friends from helping friends. Sadly Tad had
believed Zack's offer was sincere, and waited foolishly for
the job. Sam, however, was wiser. He had street smarts
enough to know a b.s.-er when he met one. He never
expected help from white men, especially in Hollywood.

Zack dreaded the slightest good will Tad or Sam might
garner due to being in an episode of "his" show. What it

was he'd lose, should they come off better than him, was
not clear. It never is. Stars often turn their backs on
former friends, friends who did nothing wrong, nothing to
deserve the cold shoulder, once success is achieved.

Tad's money supply dwindled. He eventually took
Amanda up on her offer to pay a slice of rent -- not much,
two hundred dollars a month -- which helped.

Finally Franklin found a small part in another low-
budget movie, one which paid $200+, at S.A.G. scale, each
of three and a half days. Tad needed to play a soldier
home on leave, so he received a short haircut and a
uniform. Not many lines, except there was a big argument
between family members where Tad could shout and vent his
feelings, maybe ten lines' worth. He asked Amanda to help
him with the reading prep, and then when he got the role,
with all the scenes.

It was a long drive to San Diego (the "family home,"
supposedly, a big house that just happened to be owned by
the producer who donated it cheaply for the movie). Tad
drove and paid his motel room one night (a concession he
made when asked) and then drove roundtrip each remaining
day. His agent could have forced the production to pay,
but Tad didn't want to risk the job, even by legally

demanding his rights. Franklin opposed the arrangement on principle, naturally, but saw the wisdom of Tad's well-founded concern: they could hire a San Diego actor, or someone who would take the arrangement. Either way, Tad would lose. This bargain was reached prior to contract approval, "under the table," so to speak.

He had fun, despite the long drive. The other cast members were proficient, and his yelling scene worked well. The cameraman recommended two closeups at crucial points, which the director (a woman) readily embraced after seeing Tad's intense rehearsal. For him the pain of being misunderstood, of being treated dismissively by parents, was easy to portray, having had years of experience personally. The final take saw tears flow. The crew applauded. Pent-up anger at his own selfish mother gave a stinging edge to his delivery.

The final drive back to Los Angeles presented some difficulty -- Tad was exhausted. He'd have to complain to Mr. Christian for not warning him how tough film work was compared to stage work. If anything, his teacher had implied the opposite, that stage work demanded more emotional finesse and energy than film.

The money came in at the right time, just in time to pay bills. Those credit cards! Easy to use, hard to pay. Oh well. This movie was art, in his opinion, and now he would do as Amanda suggested: get a part that wasn't necessarily art, but could bring in more money.

Franklin was greatly relieved by Tad's phone call explaining the idea, freeing up Franklin to look for "just about anything."

It had been those beautiful eyes that did the trick. Tad couldn't fight them. Her appealing look melted him, persuaded him as no realistic presentation of cold facts possibly could have. She sat beside him as he phoned Franklin, as he even repeated her words: "A little extra money can't hurt, it'll make waiting for the proper movie possible."

That night she pressed those breasts against his back, whispering how much it pleased her that he'd taken her advice. Tad fought the impulse to turn over, saying, instead, "We'll see what happens." She didn't move away for one full minute.

The "money" role Franklin found resembled *TRAPPED* in that Tad was again a robber -- this time of a convenience

store. He brandished a pistol, took the cash, jumped in a
car driven by his "girlfriend," shot a bullet in the window
as they drove off. The police caught them before long --
duh! -- and he ended up in jail, feeling anger and remorse,
completing his part. The story continued, focusing on the
girlfriend's experiences: prison time, release, drug
addiction, etc., etc., rehabilitation, relapse,
prostitution, hard times, meeting a nice guy,
rehabilitation. In the final scene she tossed a photo of
Tad in the trash, repenting of her past, sliding into the
nice guy's arms, music swelling up as the credits rolled.

To Tad's surprise *WOMAN LOST AND FOUND* became a hit.
No more interviews for Tad -- the producers offered him
crook parts, some of which he liked; by the end of six
months he'd played three crooks, earned twenty thousand
dollars, made appearances on local news entertainment
segments, dated older actresses (semi-stars) and been
approached by other agencies to leave Turner Talent. But
he didn't want to leave Franklin. He <u>did</u> want to do a big
movie with stars in it, however, and told Franklin if he
couldn't find one, he'd go to another agency that could.

But, before that, before *WOMAN LOST AND FOUND* was
released, all hell broke loose at his bungalow.

One night Amanda came in from work, claiming Vince had followed her, that she'd shaken him, but was afraid he'd show up anyway, somehow. Tad was out, but Sam dressed and stood at the door with a crowbar in his hand. Sure enough, Vince arrived. She hadn't "shaken" him. He stood at a distance, hollering at Sam to send her out. He called him "nigger."

"Get the fuck outta here, get going," Sam responded, lifting the crowbar. Amanda appeared behind him, yelling she'd call the police if he didn't leave. Vince charged, Sam struck him, Amanda ran to her phone. But Sam prevailed upon her not to call 911, to call Tad instead. Vince was moaning, conscious, outside.

"I only hit him a tap, sweetie. Don't worry. See? He's alright." She called Tad, explained as best she could, and asked Sam, "What now?"

"Nothing, nothing. This dude will split. You watch. Is Tad coming?"

"Right away." She fell into the chair, not crying, stone-faced, watching Vince struggle to his feet, outside.

"Come with me, Amanda," he begged.

"That ship has sailed, sucker," Sam replied calmly. "Beat it. If I see you again, I'll finish you off. Get outta here."

Vince relented, not doubting a bit the import of Sam's words. He backed off, toward the front gate.

"I'll sue you. What's your name?"

"You'll sue shit!" Sam advanced, Vince retreated. Two neighbors opened their front doors to look.

"No problem," Sam told them. "He's leaving."

Vince did. He went to his car, on the street, placing his hand to his head, glaring at Sam, but saying nothing more. Amanda remained inside the house. Vince drove off. Sam laughed, walked in and slammed the door, tossed the crowbar on the couch, went into the kitchen for a drink of water, brought Amanda a beer, which she refused, held her face up, and asked, "Okay, babe?"

"Yes," she said, standing, trembling, to hug him. "Thank you. Oh, thank you."

"Anytime, sweetie."

When Tad arrived he wanted to call the police, too, but Sam talked him out of it.

"We'll never see that fucker again," Sam said. Then, to Amanda, "Pardon my language."

What followed was a frustrating night for Tad. He held Amanda, in their bed, for what seemed like an hour before she could fall asleep -- even with two glassfuls of wine. She cried, some. Not much. Sam stayed up watching TV in the living room -- "on guard," as Tad expressed it, "Not for any good reason," as Sam expressed it. Sam explained his stashed crowbar this way: "somethin' my old man taught me."

But in bed with Amanda so close the fire burned, the mind resisted, the heart pounded, the emotions wavered. Tad wrestled with his needs until she slept, then relaxed. Naturally he felt proud to be a protector, even if Sam got the superseding credit.

Another unpleasant event occurred before Tad got his successful movie part. Sara came to visit, asking him to move in with her. She'd dropped her longtime boyfriend/fiancé because he'd cheated on her, and longed for the love she and Tad enjoyed during high school.

They met at a barbecue restaurant near his house. Sara admitted she'd lied about having another reason to be in L.A., making a visit with Tad "convenient."

"Sorry. I wouldn't have said it but I was scared you'd say no if you thought I only wanted to come see you."

"That makes no sense," he replied.

"Sorry again. It made sense to me."

"What am I, a monster?"

"I was scared to... put pressure on you. Or for you to perceive it that way."

"I don't," Tad said. "It's nice to see you again. Your hair looks good long." She was older looking, too, with that long brown hair, smart black blouse and skirt, bracelets on both wrists, heavy makeup.

"I got a tattoo. But don't ask to see it." She pointed to her lower abdomen. "Can't show it to you."

"Why not? I've seen you there."

"Sure, Tad. You have. Sometime -- if you come live with me." She was acting coquettish. That hadn't changed.

He ate his tri-tip sandwich, then asked her: "How's your family?"

"Fine. I'm going to college. In Fullerton, like you did."

"Cool." Tad couldn't have cared less. He'd suffered too much during their relationship, and knew not to get drawn in. She'd end up complaining how some people were mistreating her at school, how he, only, understood her, how she needed him. Sara had initially covered part of that ground after they'd sat down to order lunch. But she began once more:

"It's a pain being alone, not being with you. I shouldn't have ended it... never mind. I'm different now. I won't smother you anymore. I promise. I'll be good to you, really."

"Well, sure. But I can't just go to -- anywhere. My agent is here, the jobs are here. You know."

"Can't you drive up for that? It's not too far."

"Yes it is." Also, he didn't want to leave Amanda in the lurch. What would she do, or Sam, if he moved out? "Auditions can happen fast, you know. I should be close by." That was partly a lie, partly true. A day's delay wouldn't cause much of a problem, but the wait <u>might</u> be crucial. "They could give the part to somebody else before I got to audition."

"Why?"

"Why? I don't know. Maybe they'd be in a hurry. Maybe the thing would be starting soon, they'd be forced to decide right away."

"You with someone else, now?"

"No, no. Not really."

"Not really?" She smiled, acted coquettish. "Just off and on?"

"Not that, even. A friend. She lives with me."

"No sex?"

"Uh-uh."

"Don't like her that way? Not pretty enough?"

"It isn't that. I don't care about that. She's nice." Big boobs, he thought, but didn't say it. "You're prettier than her."

"That's nice. That was my point."

"No, I -- it isn't because of that. I mean you _are_ prettier, and yet I still like her. Oh, shit --"

"That's a compliment?"

"No, it's -- yes. You're confusing me."

"Okay. We'll drop it. I'm only asking for, say, a few months. You can decide to stay or go later."

"Later? Why would I? If I moved in I'd do it for longer than that."

She drank her Coke, feigning disinterest.

Tad said: "I know full well how good you'd be to me. I wouldn't _want_ to leave. But we'd fight, again, you'd

talk about marriage again, I'd hurt you again. I'd feel
like shit again, I'd --"

"Shut up, will you?" Tears formed in her eyes, fell
down her cheeks, clung to her chin. She whipped them off.
He said nothing more. She sighed like she used to, in high
school, so dramatic, so helplessly pathetic. Tad had never
been able to fathom the purpose of those big sighs -- were
they fake or were they real expressions of inner
consciousness?

"Please don't feel bad. I'm sorry," he said, taking
both of her hands in his, like the old days. "It could
happen, in the future. Really. I just don't want to leave
here, now. I'm getting jobs. I'm making my way. That's
all."

There was a brief ADR session (re-recording dialogue
which for whatever reason -- usually background noise
interference -- was not recorded well on the set at the
time of filming) in a sound studio, for Tad, for the
soldier-on-leave movie. He went in, spoke and yelled a
couple of times into a microphone while his scenes ran on a
screen in front of him, thanked everyone, went out the door
feeling a sense of professional accomplishment, tempted to

call Mr. Christian to describe the experience, but drove to a local coffee shop for an egg sandwich instead. Sitting at the counter Tad realized he was neglecting his other teacher, the college professor who had believed in him so, and resolved to call and meet with her to "catch up," to relate his experiences in Hollywood, to find out how she was faring without him -- jokingly, of course. She must be preparing or directing another college production. Perhaps he'd check it out later -- take Amanda and maybe Sam, or Zack, even. With their dates, of course.

Coincidentally, that evening, Amanda didn't come in until very late. Tad waited up, with Sam, both nervous but unwilling to call her cell phone. Not that she'd mind, necessarily, but her life was her life, after all. Sam went to bed at midnight. Tad turned down the TV and sat, worrying, drawing incrementally closer to reaching for the phone, until she arrived, shocked to see him in the living room:

"Hi, Tad! Why are you up so late?" She came in, tossing down her coat, smiling, looking at him with those beautiful eyes, and suddenly guessed the truth. "Oh, I should have told you before! I was on a date. I'm really sorry. Did you worry about me?"

"Yes, but it's okay." He shut off the silent TV. "Sam too. Maybe you should let us know, now that I think of it. Because, well, we wondered." He didn't mention Vince. Didn't have to. That was understood.

She knelt on the sofa, embracing him, actually kissing his cheek. "Oh, Tad. I'm stupid. I didn't think --" She stopped talking, recalling that crazy night. "Is he asleep?"

"Don't know."

"I'm going to let him know I'm alright." She stood, crossed to Sam's door, knocked gently. There was no response. "Must be asleep."

"Don't know," Tad repeated, standing, looking uncomfortably at her, wondering what to say. She supplied the words: "He's okay. I'll apologize in the morning." As she passed, going to the bathroom, she quipped, "Hope you didn't call the police."

Tad laughed out of courtesy, irritated she'd switched moods so rapidly.

"Be right out," Amanda whispered, so as not to wake Sam, and went through their bedroom door.

Of all the strange events in his recent life one of the strangest was being in bed with her that night discussing her date. Not that the date was so weird, but lying together in the dark talking about it was, at least to him.

A young doctor at the hospital, who'd asked her out before, had tried again. This time she'd accepted a late dinner, a glass of wine, a kiss at the car, even a squeeze on her behind.

"He's nice. Not married. Doctors like nurses, you know, even if I'm not really a nurse. Never finished the program. Did I tell you that?"

"Oh, yeah. I know."

"When I was with Terrence I always said no to them. But now -- why not?"

"Right."

"There's another one -- a surgeon. He's married, though. Invited me to Las Vegas once."

"And you didn't go?"

"Of course not. Are you crazy?"

"Possibly." He laughed to hide his true feelings. Then, suddenly, decided to tell her: "I'm jealous." Now Amanda laughed. "Just a little. Don't sweat it." He turned away. She didn't reply. She wanted to ask him about it, but sensed a problem, a strain in their arrangement, would develop if she did. They lay in silence for a few moments. Tad finally asked, foolishly, "You didn't mind he squeezed your butt?"

"No! So what?"

"Nothing." Tad felt weak.

She held her breath, held her voice, held her anger. It passed. When at last she spoke Amanda was feeling, instead, compassion. "Does it bother you so much?"

"Sort of. I don't want to lie."

That was the end of it. Amanda couldn't find a word that seemed appropriate, and most certainly Tad couldn't either.

After filming *WOMAN LOST AND FOUND*, Tad phoned his college professor, Clarissa Howard, and left a long message on her office voice mail. She promptly returned his call. Mrs. Howard was thirty-five, pretty, and full of life. She feared Tad vaguely, for no good reason, other than his unpredictability on stage which indicated possible dangerousness offstage. That only materialized once, when Tad failed to show up for a rehearsal of *U.S.A.*, having accidentally sideswiped a parked car and driven off. He didn't want to be on the road the rest of the day for fear a witness had described his car to the police. So he didn't go to the school. Clarissa was quite angry, but they made up, so to speak, at the next rehearsal.

He'd gotten his fender repaired, and painted, and gradually lost whatever guilt feelings the "hit-and-run" had caused. Clarissa recommended he return to the street of the accident, but he lied, saying he couldn't recall the spot. She never quite trusted him after that, but admired his talents nevertheless.

"What are you up to these days?" she asked on the phone.

"Just finished a film -- for the money -- and now I'm looking for a good job. Got a few small roles, nothing special. I'll let you know when -- if -- the films come out."

"Please do that. Are you enjoying it?"

"Pretty much. Not as fun as our play, though. They work so fast!"

"I know. Good luck. I have to scoot, sorry. We'll talk longer the next time."

"Oh -- okay. You doing alright?"

"Oh yes. Busy. I'll call you when there's more time."

"Great. Take care of yourself."

"You too. Goodbye."

"Goodbye," he said, and they both hung up. Only then did Tad remember he'd wanted to visit her. Have to arrange that another time.

She sat alone in her office at school, thinking of their play, of the good response to it, of the long struggle preparing the cast for opening night. Now she was repeating the process with a new production, a new cast (except for two actresses from *U.S.A.*). Clarissa partly regretted Tad had left school. She would have cast him again, no doubt about it. Possibly he'd come back, but that seemed doubtful. She believed he would succeed.

More weeks elapsed. Vince never showed up. Sam got a new female "friend." Amanda went out with her doctor again, once even staying out all night. She phoned the guys ahead of time, now. Tad remained jealous. Zack's series was indeed "picked up" for another season, although he never called with the news -- Tad learned it from Franklin. The four thousand for *WOMAN LOST AND FOUND* didn't last long, after taxes. The producers told Franklin they were pushing for an early release; they were extremely happy with the movie.

Tad spent part of his money on car repairs (someday, he told himself, he would have a new car) and he bought a hose to use in front of the bungalow, and purchased new clothes (not many).

His mother tried to talk him into flying to Portland for a visit, but he begged off. He hated visiting her. Always a hassle. He'd have to soon, though -- she didn't brook much delay where her wants were concerned.

Franklin said he was looking for a "special" movie role -- he didn't use the word "art." Amanda suggested he do another movie "for the money," no matter how bad it was.

"I understand your point of view," he told her, "but for me it isn't that easy. My plan was to be an artist, not a greedy hack."

He didn't realize that characterization hurt her feelings until she turned bright red and looked down. They were in the living room, on a Saturday. Sam was out.

"I know you didn't mean it that way," he continued. "I'm only trying to say -- well -- it's art for art's sake. You know, not parts that <u>say</u> <u>nothing</u>, that just titillate, just cover the same old ground."

"I know," she replied. She stood up from the couch and went to the kitchen. He felt bad, and followed her. She was at the sink, doing nothing, and Tad put his arms around her waist; she turned.

"I'll make another one, regardless. If my agent can't find anything suitable, and probably he can't, I'll play whatever part I can get. You taught me that." He kissed her forehead.

Amanda put her arms around him. The silence was deafening. Neither one moved for a few seconds until Tad reached up to stroke her hair. She kissed him on the cheek and disengaged from his embrace, giggling, saying impulsively:

"Trying to get me excited?"

"No. Was I?"

"As if you didn't know."

"I didn't." He followed her into the living room, watched her sit on the couch with her legs up, her arms over her knees. "Doesn't your doctor take care of you?"

"Take care of me?"

"Yeah." He sat in his old chair, laughing to cover his embarrassment.

"If you mean what I think you mean, the answer is no."

"Oh, I thought he did."

She stared at Tad, suspecting in her heart that he was insane. "You've been sitting there thinking that all this time?"

"Uh, yeah," he admitted reluctantly.

"And Sam too, I suppose?"

"Yeah. You spent the night out with the dude, didn't you? Come on --"

"So? Well, yes, one night we did it, okay? Are you happy? One night! Not all the time like you're thinking." She started to leave, again, but he said:

"Wait. I'm sorry. Are you mad?"

"No. But... it's none of your business."

"Right. You asked me, so I told you what I thought."

She sat down again and smiled at him. "Jealous?"

"I'm jealous, I'm sorry to say."

"Don't be sorry."

His phone rang, but he let it ring. They sat listening to it.

"Maybe I should move out," she said, finally.

"Uh-uh. No. We're cool."

She smiled again. "Sure?"

"Sure I'm sure. Everything is cool, isn't it?

"Well, yes, but..." She looked down.

"What?"

"I wish you would hold me at night."

Tad's movie came out, and while he was only in the first quarter of it, local press not only mentioned him but did so favorably, in reviews. Except one said he seemed to be imitating Nicolas Cage, which Tad had not been attempting to do -- at least not consciously. But he could see the reason for the criticism. He promised himself to make a conscious effort not to do that in the future. If anything, he'd go more toward Jack Nicholson (if he could).

Of course Mr. Christian had warned against imitation -- "Go down your own path. Get the character's mannerisms from <u>inside</u>, after you take on the outer behavior." Good advice. But not always easy to follow. Mannerisms usually were one's own, and occasionally were assumed from observation of others, on film, or off. In his early "exercises" in Mr. Christian's class Tad had acted like Leonardo DiCaprio in *TITANIC* -- jumpy but self-assured. Later he dropped that when classmates began to mention the similarity. Finally he tried to use himself in the mix --

after finding the character through the requirements of the story. But that was difficult and scary, for some reason.

The female lead in *WOMAN LOST AND FOUND* received the greatest praise, deservedly. She was stunning, and a major reason audiences bought tickets. Of course the movie was all about her, so when a TV critic mentioned "Oscar-worthy," it seemed right. Any veneration would rub off on Tad (he hoped), since many of his scenes were with her.

Once the film caught on, parts became easier to get. Crook parts, that was. One, in fact, was fairly artistic, and Tad did it for less money than he might have -- a thousand dollars less -- over Franklin's objections.

Sleeping beside Amanda, holding her, watching her heavy-lidded eyes close into slumber, turned out to be less exacting than he'd predicted. Luckily he was able to keep his passion at bay. It was the sympathy he felt, no doubt, which permitted restraint. She didn't need another man taking advantage of her. Unknown to him, Amanda was feeling sexual, but suppressed it, also. She didn't want to ruin the existing situation. At least, she feared sex would likely lead to complications, even conflict. So she fought her feelings.

Sam, infrequently, joked in reference to them sleeping together, implying they were "doing it," that they weren't fooling him any. But he couldn't figure out why they would pretend so much. Crazy, he concluded.

"Don't hold the noise down for <u>my</u> benefit," he quipped once. "Means nothing to me."

"Noise?" Tad asked innocently.

"White folks don't make noise, I guess."

Tad laughed out loud at that. "I'm telling you, man, you've got it all wrong."

"Right. In that case, you are one dumb son-of-a-bitch."

Other times Sam almost believed it. He never saw them kiss, he never caught them at anything. One evening he brought his new friend, Kelly, to dinner. Amanda volunteered to cook. The four of them had a good time, and Sam explained the arrangement to Kelly. Amanda didn't bat an eye, but Tad was chagrinned, somehow, shrugging it off.

"They've got will power, I'll say that," Sam intoned. "I kinda admire them."

"Should we try it?" Kelly asked.

"Please, God, no," Sam responded.

After coffee, sit-ups, a shower, a few spiritual affirmations read from a pamphlet, Tad watched the morning news, keeping the sound down so as not to disturb Amanda. She wasn't getting up early anymore.

The news dampened Tad's optimism. The war in Iraq, the federal deficit, the bickering by commentators. What buttressed his optimism was having a hit movie in the theatres and a script to study, a "start date" around the corner, and therefore, money coming in. But the rest of the country, the world? Saddening indeed. His father, dead now, had been a Republican, a supporter of Reagan, born at the beginning of the Eisenhower era, long before Bush and his cronies flipped Conservatism on its proud head. Reagan had been okay, Tad felt, except people pointed out the national debt soared during those seemingly prosperous years. People also said Clinton had fixed the economy, started paying down that debt, and encouraged job creation, until his enemies went after him for lying under oath. He left a "legacy," they said, of economic gain and personal embarrassment. Now we had a "war against terror" and economic "uncertainty." Tad shut off the TV, not wanting to hear about the increasing casualty numbers in Iraq, because every time he heard them he wondered how Iraq had become part of the "war against terror." Let the smart experts figure it out. He had to learn his lines and practice them as much as he could.

Amanda was sleeping peacefully. He took a look at her through the bedroom door, closed it again, and headed to the kitchen. There he opened his script and ate a bowlful of 'Special K,' mumbling his lines as he read them over and over. Screw the news.

But his father's memory returned, so Tad closed the script and sat in painful silence. A good person, teaching his sons discipline and morality, some of which stuck, and trout fishing, which didn't. His father had died of lung cancer at the early age of 49, leaving a moderate bank account and very few unpaid debts. Tad's older brother Arthur lived in San Francisco, working as a city employee. Married at a young age, and divorced already, Arthur seldom phoned or visited Tad (apparently satisfied with Tad's occasional trips to the City by the Bay), exhibiting superficial friendliness, but down on the acting profession, down on life in general, down on Tad for harboring bitterness toward their mother -- a "monster" in Tad's view, a "misunderstood woman" in Arthur's.

But their father had been a fair man; he provided, he set aside time to be with his boys, he took them camping, he encouraged Boy Scout ethics, hard work over expediency, love over retribution, religion over secularism -- he was a believer, their mother was not. She called Christianity "stupid." Of course, he was weak, he let her mistreat the boys, he let her buy expensive clothes for herself, he let her lie manipulatively, and simply laughed it off when Tad went to him with the evidence of her deceptions. For instance, she didn't like the dog Tad's father had brought them, so she announced the authorities had taken it away, one day, when the boys were at school and she was in the house alone, that their neighbor had been bitten and the dog was the culprit. Years later Tad discovered the factual errors, that the law was not so harsh, that she had initiated the crisis by calling up to have their "crazy" dog returned to the pound, and later, to be euthanized. It was all in the records at the dog pound -- Tad had checked, finally. When confronted she only could say to him, defiantly: "So have you forgiven me?" His brother had told Tad to "forget it." But he didn't -- he loved that dog.

Kiko called, again, to run the next morning. He'd been working on location in Alaska, of all places.

"Sure, man, let's do it," Tad replied. "I'll meet you at seven, okay?"

"Okay, dude."

He went back to studying his part, but Amanda came into the kitchen, seeking coffee, so they talked until she left for work. She overcame the temptation to kiss him goodbye, then regretted it later. All day she thought about him, reinforcing her commitment to no sex, steeling herself for the evening to come. Her friend the doctor asked her to a movie on the weekend. She accepted.

TRAPPED finally came out, to mediocre reviews, but box office business was lively, temporarily. Tad's name was mentioned on the local news channel, although the star, the bank robber "boss," got the most credit, such as it was. People like action, shooting, fast getaways, blah blah blah, Tad thought.

Amanda saw it with Doctor Ruskin. She told him Tad was her "roommate," rather than "bedmate." But that night was especially difficult for her, energized and excited by seeing Tad on film. Luckily for her he'd been asleep when she came to bed. The doctor had asked her to pass on a compliment to Tad, which she did in the morning. The oddness of the situation was obvious to both Amanda and Tad, but unspoken.

In reaction, Tad took out an actress from his last movie. She was over eighteen -- in fact, she was over forty. Dawn Draper, a star whose career was 'going south.' She looked great in makeup, but not as good without it. Not that Tad cared. She was fun, full of stories about her early movies and Golden Globe nomination. They went to a club in Hollywood to hear a punk rock band from the eighties. Dawn knew the lead singer, so they went backstage afterward, then to the singer's house in Malibu for drinks. A few of the partygoers took cocaine, but Dawn and Tad declined offers to indulge. They danced and drank, and kissed in a big soft chair, and Tad suggested advancing the romance at her place, but Dawn objected, "for now," smiling lusciously, thanking him for his "flattering proposal." He tried again at her door, but she pushed him away, asking, "What are you, half my age?"

"No," he lied. "Anyway, so what if I was, which I'm not saying I am, so what?"

"No offense, sweetheart," she said, leaning up to kiss him on the mouth, and pushing him away again, playfully. "I've got pilates in the morning, anyway. See?" She flexed her smooth but strong bicep. "Maybe I'll show you my muscles sometime. But not tonight."

He couldn't think of a reply. She entered her house, so he said "I'll call you."

"Good. Thanks for a great evening."

"Me too. You too, I mean," he said awkwardly. She laughed as she closed the door. He went to his car feeling deflated yet hopeful. Show me your muscles? But why not tonight? Was there another man in the house? Not according to her. No boyfriend, no husband. One son, an aspiring actor, living elsewhere. Tad hoped her son was younger than he was.

Amanda was out when he finally climbed into bed. She'd called Sam, who left a note. "A new dude," he'd written. In bed Tad decided that the routine phone call was unnecessary, now. None of them thought Vince would cause any more problems. He'd talk with them about dropping the requirement.

He masturbated, dreading and wishing simultaneously Amanda would walk in on him. She didn't.

Since Amanda was off work, the three of them, with Kelly, went to Universal Theme Park the next day. Tad and Amanda refused to go on the many rides -- both nervous about the "violence" of them, as Tad termed it. But Sam and Kelly loved the rides, and ridiculed their fears.

They ate at one of the many food shops, this one with a replica of the *JAWS* shark, "Bruce," displayed outside. Tad and Amanda described their dates of the previous evening. Kelly laughed at them, and asked: "Are you guys on a date now? Or is that forbidden?"

Sam chimed in, "It's a date, only they won't admit it."

"We're friends," Amanda said.

Tad agreed, "Yeah. This isn't really a date."

"You're fooling yourselves," Sam said. "Two birds on a wire acting like strangers to each other. Get over it."

Amanda shook her head, but Tad wondered. He turned to her and asked, "Are we fooling ourselves? I don't know. Do you like me more than as a friend?" When she didn't speak, he added, "For me, you know, I wonder."

"Now that's what I'm talking about," Sam remarked, loudly. "Two birds on a wire."

Still Amanda didn't speak. She was afraid to say what was in her heart. Tad sensed it, and joked, "You better be careful, Sam. We might kick you out!"

Sam shouted, "Bullshit." Kelly hit him on the arm. He glared at her. "What?"

"Leave them alone," Kelly demanded. "It's their decision."

"Oh, hell. Let's go to the *BACKDRAFT* show," he said, standing. "I heard it was <u>hot</u>." He laughed, concealing his embarrassment, cutting through the seriousness.

The *BACKDRAFT* exhibit <u>was</u> hot, with fires blasting up at the audience in unnerving proximity, the heat of the controlled blazes prompting screams and sudden backward steps. Outside in the cool air, the four of them decided on the next activity (the tram tour), never mentioning their recent conversation again. But anyone observing them would have thought: 'a black couple and a white couple,' because they consciously paired up, oblivious to appearance, each with their own personal tremulous feelings, each with their own private thoughts -- Kelly hoping she and Sam had a future, Amanda controlling her increasing fondness for Tad, Tad confused and torn, Sam wishing he'd kept his big mouth shut.

That night in bed both Tad and Amanda restrained themselves. She, afraid of the certain ramifications, he, conflicted and waiting for a clue. In the next room no uncertainty constrained its occupants -- they made coital "noise," and the others heard it.

Meanwhile, during the following week, Dr. Ruskin took Amanda to lunch and proposed marriage. She turned him down, citing her youth, her appreciation of personal freedom, and finally, the main reason: she didn't love him. He hated that.

"You'll learn to love me. Take a chance, and see," he told her.

"No, honey, really. I like you, but I'm not in love with you."

That settled that. Dr. Ruskin stopped asking her out. Another doctor she'd dated took up the slack, asking Amanda to dinner and, unusually, dancing. She enjoyed that. He was a calm, fortyish gentleman, an anesthesiologist. But Amanda craved excitement -- he offered none. She discussed him with Tad, but after two conversations gave up. Dr. Billingsly failed to provoke Tad's jealous side. So she had sex with him and informed Tad about it the next day.

"Good," he said. "Now I don't feel guilty. Not doing it with you."

"Not doing it with me?" she asked, her voice rising.

"That can't be a surprise. You've -- you've wanted to, haven't you?"

She said nothing.

"It felt like it. Maybe I'm wrong."

She laughed. "So self-confident!"

"Sorry. I'm not, I only felt it. You didn't?"

"Didn't _what_?"

Tad looked away. They were in the kitchen at the breakfast table. "Like, you... feel hot in bed. Restless."

"And?"

"It could indicate desire, I don't know." He looked back at her. "No?"

"No. You've got quite an imagination. Probably _you're_ the one with all the raging desire."

"Okay, I admit it."

"You admit it?" Her voice rose again.

"Uh-huh." Once more he glanced away.

"Could have fooled me."

"I was trying to," he said.

Amanda laughed. "All this time?"

"No, not all this time. Okay... recently."

She stood and went to the counter for no good reason, other than to escape his eyes. Tad was relieved to have told her, but fearful of her reaction. Would she move out?

She kept her back turned and said, "I wouldn't mind, you know."

The thrill that passed suddenly throughout his body exceeded any he'd felt in his life. But he was immobile. She finally turned to face him. "Cat got your tongue?"

They made the most of the two nights remaining before he left for location on his next job -- to Wyoming. Then they spoke on the phone often. Tad was playing a bad cult member who killed his adopted teenage son in a shootout when the FBI raided their compound. The director urged him to act mean, and he complied, but it was difficult work, as happy as he was to be linked, at last, with Amanda, sexually and emotionally. The "son" had turned informant, and Tad's character flipped out, shooting him from behind after learning of the betrayal.

Wyoming was beautiful -- "big sky" country -- and Tad's heart was soaring, regardless of his character's nefarious behavior. Amanda said she loved him, that she was waiting for him, that she wouldn't forget to take the "pill." He'd made a friend, Frank, who was playing the cult's second-in-command. Frank wanted Tad to join him on his next film. Franklin checked it out -- a drag-racing plot with Frank as the drag-racer, Tad as one of his mechanics. By the end of filming *MASTERMIND*, Franklin had secured Tad's role in *BURNING RUBBER*, and all was well.

Meanwhile Amanda politely declined Dr. Billingsly's repeated invitations. He was hurt. She had a "boyfriend," she said. "These things happen."

At the airport leaving Wyoming the crew and several cast members said goodbye, and Frank told a racist joke. On the plane Tad decided he'd have to live with his racism until the completion of *BURNING RUBBER*, and cast aside their friendship. Some were like that in Hollywood, he knew. Anti-black, anti-gay, anti-Semitic -- in spite of Hollywood's supposed liberal leanings. Tad himself harbored some negative attitudes, and knew Sam resented whites -- at least, the powerful 'secretly racist' ones. There was little Tad could do about it -- everyone had "facts" to point to which confirmed their prejudices, on the surface and occasionally well below. Weren't there a lot of blacks in prison, and Jews successfully climbing corporate ladders, and hadn't homosexuals bothered him repeatedly on movie sets and at parties? Weren't women criticized as weak, by men, and men criticized as pigs, by women?

Tad was depressed by the time his plane landed at LAX, and after getting his bags and taking a cab to the house, he forced his mind away from humankind's intolerance toward a mental picture of Amanda's eyes, her sweet smile, toward, ultimately, her vagina. He unpacked, he called her at work; he said, at last, he "loved" her (did he?) and popped a Pacifico, awaiting her return later in the evening.

They hired a Salvadorian housekeeper, since money from the crook parts and the Wyoming movie put Tad, at least, in a fair financial position. The three bungalow inhabitants had tired of doing housework. Tad drove his 4-door Honda Accord out to Malibu nearly once a month, now, parking, then walking, near the beach, to breathe the fresh air, study the blue horizon, dream of owning a big house there, having parties, sleeping in, running on the wet sand, reading scripts until lunch, calling Franklin with pleas for good jobs, watching TV, diving into library books

during the afternoon, catching the "moment lost" with a
glass of beer and perhaps a dog by his side, watching (both
of them) the darkening sky, praising God for fortune,
hearing Amanda (or someone) fixing dinner, eating it on the
deck with salt air mingling with food smells -- all these
ideas came easily to his mind until Tad returned to
reality, drove into the city, shopped for groceries, made
it to the bungalow and forgot about blue Malibu.

Two of the bad guy movies had been released, advancing
his career (according to Franklin) even without garnering
box office success. He made the hotrod movie with Frank.
It might be "big," Franklin said after viewing an early
'rough cut,' like *WOMAN LOST AND FOUND*, and job offers
sporadically passed Tad's way. Where was the major part?
he sometimes asked Franklin. "Oh, it's coming," he was
told. But it didn't. "Too much competition," Franklin
said. "Be patient."

The shock was when Amanda broke the awful news (for
Tad) that she wanted to move into her own apartment. Not
break up with him, really, she said, but "partly." Her
reason? Need for space, for a potential husband, for a
"change" in things. Actually, she said, she didn't love

him. Could he understand that? Of course, he said. He didn't "actually" love her, but he would sure miss those breasts, that vagina, those stunning eyes. He only mentioned the last part. But he'd see them (her eyes), she insisted, if he wanted to. That was the way it went, and three days after she moved out, Tad turned twenty-three, drank seven beers, briefly cried in bed, and longed for his college days.

As a matter of fact, his college days had been easy and fun, in spite of, or perhaps due to, the reality he faced of having to work and take fewer classes, extending the normal two-year Associate of Arts degree program into three years. Even though his mother had the money ($25,000 in a savings account), she wouldn't turn loose of but a few thousand to help him along. Greedy, selfish, heartless, in his opinion.

The fun part of college was the development of friendships, parties, acting classes, plays, even studying (when the subject matter suited him -- philosophy, psychology, English, Journalism). The _ease_ was manifested in the slower schedule, the ability to pass less attractive classes (Biology, Classical History, Physical Education, and, of course, Algebra). Drugs he avoided, for no

apparent reason other than possibly Tad's awareness that
his mind was his main asset, something not to be toyed with
recklessly, and that Sara had literally grimaced at the
idea of drug use -- hard or soft -- which influenced Tad's
"just say no" decision. And Mr. Christian, his friendship
continuing after high school, disdained any and all use of
drugs except caffeine and nicotine, if Tad so chose. The
former he did, the latter he didn't.

Mornings without Amanda stung almost as sharply as
nights without her. Tad fought the urge to call, to take
her out, only succumbing on a very few occasions. She'd
made her decision. He'd live with it. Why force her into
contact she'd found unfulfilling? Someone else would enjoy
her company, her gentleness, her huge breasts, her serious
work ethic, her tender kisses, her passionate lovemaking.
Love. She didn't "love" him. What was love anyway? More
than Tad could imagine. More than his parents had had.
Possibly it was something like what he and Sara had felt
the first year of their romance: a painful need to be with
the other person, a joyous lightness being with them, a
constant adventure.

Zack met him accidentally at the talent agency one
day; Tad and he hung out at Carrows, talking politics

(campaign finance reform) and acting (Stanislavski),
agreeing to go to a local play (*THE CHERRY ORCHARD*) soon,
complaining about the casting process, the mean directors,
the scene-stealers, the general dearth of creativity, the
wisdom of Mr. Christian, the disappointing array of current
movies, the talent of Edward Norton, the talent of Annette
Bening, the power or lack thereof of Franklin, the detached
effervescence of Destiny, one of his female clients (Tad
had met her only once, Zack had worked with her on his
series), the humor of George Carlin, the use of the word
"Irregardless," the issue of illegal immigration, the issue
of terrorism, the fact that both Tad and Zack had been
approached by gay makeup artists, that the dream of an
Academy Award or an Emmy grew ever more distant as time
went on, that making money was more important than it used
to be, that climate change was real, that UFOs might be,
that God's ways were mysterious. For instance, why doesn't
He answer every prayer? <u>Can't</u>, Zack said, because, hey,
two teams can't win the same football game. Right. Then
how does He decide which prayer to answer? Don't know,
Zack said, but we're supposed to pray and not lose heart.
Do you? Tad asked. Yes, I can if I make myself. Don't

you? I can if I make myself. That's the answer, then,
Zack replied. They left the restaurant, vaguely satisfied.

Frank was good in *BURNING RUBBER*, both as a local
hotrodder and, as the story progressed, a champion drag-
racer. The dragsters were loud and technically dangerous,
but Frank had complained when the production insurance
policy forbade him from driving them in the race sequences.
Tad had run around pretending to fix this and that, working
on repairs before the big race. It wasn't art, but he did
enjoy the role, to an extent. His favorite line was: "If
you won't do it my way, you can kiss my ass," shouted at
Frank in the 'racing team' trailer. He'd pushed Frank in
the chest and stormed out, leaving him at the door shouting
"You're fired!"

In the final scene, the big race, Tad was photographed
on the sidelines, watching his former "employer" win,
anyway, without his mechanical expertise, a look of pain
and happiness on his face. The reviews barely mentioned
him, however -- Frank getting all the acclaim. But the box
office was okay, and within two weeks of release Franklin
had an offer for Tad for another youth picture -- the part
of a mechanic, again, who gets beat up by a gang of petty

thieves who are attempting to mug a wealthy couple in their driveway. The gang surrounds the car before the security gate closes, and Tad's character sees this from the street. He has to climb a fence to get to the driveway, and "foolishly" tries to stop the robbery. The gang escapes, after beating him up, and later confronts Tad's character, but he's saved by the police at the last minute.

Franklin had recommended Zack for a policeman's part, and Destiny as his wife. She got the part, but not Zack. The producers picked a bigger "name," so Zack, in spite of his series, was rejected. Nevertheless, Tad wavered about accepting the small crummy role, and only relented when he thought of Amanda's advice to build up his career and be artistically selective <u>later</u>.

The salary was very good for such a short role -- five thousand -- and the two fight scenes were fun. A stunt double, dressed as Tad, hair combed like Tad, performed a major portion of the action. The double looked similar enough for the quick cuts to match together -- and Tad learned how to throw movie punches -- missing but still lining up with the camera to appear to be authentic "hits." A stunt coordinator observed every move closely, informing the director if the "punches" were "missed" -- i.e., not looking as if contact were being made. No one was injured, not even Tad's stunt double, who received many "kicks" and "punches" by the gang members, some accidentally making contact.

Climbing the fence wasn't easy -- the director allowed Tad to do it on film, after the coordinator showed Tad the procedure. What made it difficult was the speed required for dramatic effect -- no slow careful climb and jump would do. After three takes it was done satisfactorily, although Tad hurt his ankle in the final drop. A nurse packed it in ice and he sat in his dressing cubicle pondering the drift his career had taken: action, violence, limited dialogue.

Almost before he knew it the job was over, and Tad spoke with Destiny when he was leaving the set. She was in the makeup trailer.

"I heard you hurt yourself," she said from her chair. "Are you alright?"

"Kind of sprained it, but the pain isn't much. First time I ever got hurt on a job."

"Really?" She was smiling at him via the mirror in front of her as the female makeup artist applied eye shadow. "I've been injured. Once. My back." She laughed. "I fell off the arm of a chair. It was on purpose, but the fall was too great."

"Sorry to hear that." Tad didn't know what else to say. Destiny was pretty, but, as Zack had said, "distant."

"Well, see you again sometime," he finally said. "Hope we can actually have a scene or something together, sometime." He backed up, toward the door. She smiled and nodded, turning toward him, causing the makeup woman to stop, her eyebrow pencil poised inches from Destiny's face.

Tad climbed out of the trailer, closing the door, hoping she truly meant to work with him again. She was a very good actress, and he felt attracted to her, in addition. Outside the trailer he felt sad, though. She probably had a boyfriend.

He carried his backpack to his car, saying goodbye to the prop man who was passing by: "See you, Danny!"

"Are you through?"

"Yep."

Danny took the time to stop and shake his hand. "Nice working with you," he said.

"Same here," Tad replied. He went to his car and climbed in, the sadness enveloping him. Would he ever see any of these people again? Maybe, maybe not. Destiny,

sure, because she was Franklin's client. But the others?
Who knew? It made him melancholy, the awareness that this
intense experience could end so abruptly, with such
finality, never to be resumed.

Sam and he watched *KEY LARGO*, on Tad's recommendation,
but Sam didn't like it as much as he'd expected. Too
white, he said. Tad asked, "So what everyone is white --
can't you appreciate the acting?"

"Look here now," Sam responded, drinking a beer,
putting his bare feet on the coffee table, waving his hand
suddenly. "All those talented folks don't help me none.
Getting jobs in this town may be easy for white folks with
talent, but me? Second-rate parts, and scarce at that, get
it? Pushers, convicts, cops who don't talk, get it? Maybe
musicians, now and then."

"You never played a musician."

"Look here, that's not the point. Roles for bros are
<u>scarce</u>, you know what I'm sayin'?"

Tad turned down an interview for another film, but
said nothing to Sam, who would have called him "sick." But
the script was bad, the role was dumb, the title even

dumber: *BURIED IN THE BACKYARD*. It bothered him, that title, for a reason he would shortly discover. Anyway he had enough cash to wait for a better part -- for a few months.

He ran with Kiko in the morning twice a week, he slept in the empty bed, he called Mr. Christian, he read a couple of books, he took an actress from one of his movies to dinner at Sizzler, he reminded Zack again about *THE CHERRY ORCHARD*, but they never went to see it, he did sit-ups, he watched the housekeeper work, he remembered to go to the dentist, he fought the impulse to call Amanda, then gave in and spoke with her. She said her roommate wanted to meet him, could he come over some weekend? He did.

Margie was about 30, he guessed. Plump. Short black hair. Seemed crazy, but nice. They had lunch at her house in North Hollywood, where Amanda lived, now ("Closer to the hospital"). Margie talked about her work at the Regression Institute ("Never heard of it?") and raved about Rosalind Russell, an actress from the 40's and 50's.

"My favorite is a movie she made with Cary Grant -- *HIS GIRL FRIDAY*. Ever see it?"

"No," Tad replied. "Good?"

"Excellent! Let's rent it, I'll watch it with you guys."

"Sure," he said, but as it turned out, they never did. Amanda sat on the floor on big cushions. The living room was dark, with two candles on a low table, curtains drawn. Margie said she liked it that way: "Soothing."

"What happens at the Institute?" he asked. All she'd said was they helped people with emotional problems.

"Well, it's like Primal Therapy. You go back to painful past memories and feel them all over again and free yourself of the trauma. Trauma stays with you inside, you know."

"Sure," he said. "How do you do it, though? Hypnotism?"

"No way! You breathe deeply for a few minutes, and the therapist leads you, by questions, back to bad experiences. Guides you. And after a while the feelings just express themselves. You cry and yell and cuss and cry some more. Want to try it?"

"Me?"

"Yes."

"Did you?" he asked Amanda.

"Sure she did," Margie said.

"How was it?"

"Well," Amanda hesitated. "I couldn't really feel much. But I will say it scared me."

"She just blocked. We'll get to it next time. I have a cellar with soundproofing. We can do it here -- you don't have to go to the Institute."

Tad was wary. "Can't you lose control?"

"That's the whole fucking idea!" Margie exclaimed. "<u>Lose</u> it, feel the pain. Never heard of Primal Therapy?"

He hadn't, and shook his head, but asked, "Don't you, I don't know, hold grudges against people then? Say I got beat up in elementary school, for instance, and relived it, and then I'd hold a grudge, even more than I do, against the two bullies."

"Wow. Two bullies! No, you get <u>free</u> of it, free from the lingering anger and the hurt. I'm serious. You see, the problem is we hold things in, painful stuff, bad memories. That's what lingers. When we pull it up and fully feel it we can let it go for good."

"Yeah?"

"I'm serious." She nodded, leaning back in her chair. "Lots of clients report that."

"How much do you charge per session?" he asked.

"Thirty-five dollars, if it's just me, here, downstairs. But seventy at the clinic. Want to try it?"

"Well, can it help my acting?"

"Sure! You might be holding back, when you act, you might have subconscious reservations that limit you. I have a couple of clients in the profession."

"And it helped them?"

"Sure. Amanda could report more emotional freedom if she would get in touch with her trauma. She didn't go deep enough the last time."

"It's scary," Amanda admitted. Tad looked at her.

"Scary?"

"You don't <u>want</u> to relive stuff," she explained. "I was afraid. I started sobbing and just stopped. But I'll do it again. I'll get there."

"What was the trauma, if you'll say?" he asked her.

"Just something. An attack. A physical attack."

"Really?"

"Don't ask her, Tad," Margie said. "She doesn't want to talk about it."

"Oh, okay."

Then Margie leaned forward. "<u>Were</u> you beat up by bullies?"

"Yeah."

"That's a great place to start. What happens is, you remember it, you breathe deeply for a while, I put my hands on your stomach, the feelings come up, and you relive the pain. Okay?"

"Now?"

"Why not?"

He looked at Amanda in the flickering candlelight. She was smiling with encouragement.

"There's worse than that," he finally said.

"What?" Margie asked excitedly.

"It -- it happened a long time ago, after the bullies. I can't recall it very well."

"Now we're on to something," Margie exuded. "Come on, let's go downstairs."

The initial session lasted for twenty minutes. Mostly Tad breathed, Margie pressed on his stomach, telling him to picture the bullies, asked him what was the cause of the conflict, how it felt, where he was at the time, etc., etc. He didn't get too far at first, but recalling the pushing, the twisting of his arms behind, the tripping, the falling in the playground, the knees in his back, aroused his anger and fear. He cried a bit, and Margie urged; the bullies'

words returned as if yesterday: "Punk!" -- "Queer!" --
"Rat!" He'd told on them, at school, how they'd been
taking his lunch from his lunchbox, by force, and
intimidation, day after day, swearing to "pound" him if he
told. The punches to the back of his head had hurt the
worst, and Tad let loose an awful yell in the little
soundproofed basement, shocking himself. Margie only
smiled and patted him as he gasped for air. It was over.
That is, for that session.

He paid her the money, went to his apartment,
collapsed on his bed, and slept for an hour, later getting
up to eat and think about the experience. He did feel
better, actually.

The following day Tad sensed the depression Margie had
predicted ("natural"). He reviled those two boys, felt sad
he'd been treated so badly, that his parents suggested he
was "exaggerating," that he'd hidden it from the school's
administrators, that he'd avoided the boys in the future,
that he'd stopped bringing his lunchbox (leaving it in
bushes on the way to school), that he'd been a "wimp," in
his view. The depression transformed into plain

unhappiness, and he showed up at Margie's two days later, ready for more.

Amanda was at the hospital, at work. He and Margie talked out on her porch for a few minutes, he telling her further details, she cautioning against "talking it away," but then seeing in his eyes the rising emotion, letting it build, taking him downstairs, at last, to lead him through it. There was more pain to be felt due to the attack, the humiliation, the lunchbox hiding, the fear of more retaliation ("We'll kill you if you fink!"). He yelled, he gasped for air, he flopped around on the carpeted floor, Margie touched his stomach and his face, saying "Good," "Good," "You poor boy," "Let it out," "Feel it." He sobbed, he moaned, he screamed: "I hate them!"

Later, once again, the exhaustion, the sadness, the painful revelations: his post-attack disinclination to anger anyone, his fear of participating in contact sports, of, even, carrying anything which might be a target for thieves -- all resultant behavior adapted into Tad's life after that event. Now, Margie insisted, those adaptations would fall away, he would be more like "himself," the person he was "meant to be," because that altered behavior, a seemingly smart idea to a ten-year-old, would not, now, to a twenty-three-year-old, be necessary -- if it ever was necessary.

She outlined it to him during his next visit: "To protect ourselves from pain, we adjust our actions, subconsciously, in an attempt to avoid another bad experience, no matter how unlikely that experience might be. The pain you were forced to undergo triggered a survival mechanism -- avoiding upsetting anyone, no matter how justified you were in your mind."

"Wow. I wasn't aware of it at the time."

"Right." They were on the porch again, a week after the second session. He had more money in his pocket, he was willing to venture into the dark past once more. The sadness had turned into relief, the fears dissolving, the anguish caused by the attack vanishing. But a new memory was surfacing, the one he had spoken of before -- "something else. I can't recall it exactly."

They tried it again. He lay on the floor, he breathed deeply, repeatedly, she put her hands on his stomach, she asked him, "Were you beat up another time, is that it?"

He couldn't answer. The memory fled, it returned, it fled again.

"This is bad," he said.

"Take your time. Breathe."

All he could see was a twisted face, a madman. Tad was on his back, in grass. The man punched him, yelling "Turn over!" The memory fled; Tad whimpered, wept, and at last yelled. The memory returned.

"No," he'd told the twisted face. The face smiled, revealing a broken tooth.

"Turn over," it ordered again.

Tad screamed, he flopped on the carpet, Margie rubbed his belly. He groaned and cried. "No," he repeated in the cellar, and to the face. Strong fingers enclosed his throat. He was twelve years old, in the backyard of a friend's house -- no, the friend's grandmother's house. The man sat on Tad's legs, punching and choking him. "Turn over or --"

"Stop it!" He was punched again. Blood came to his lips, he spat at the face, which grew more hostile, meaner, not smiling now.

"Alright, then I'll kill you," the face said, grimacing horribly, the hands at Tad's throat, squeezing.

In the cellar he screamed, choked, sat up, looked at Margie, and whispered, "I can't, I can't do it anymore."

"Okay," she said. "Relax. It's okay. You don't have to."

But of course, he did, the following day. They brought the emotion up, the stark memory, the painful punches to the face, the hands on his throat, the weight of the madman on his body, the weakness of his position. It was as if his mind had stored every detail, and those details vividly returned.

Tad was in the sixth grade, toward the last of the year. The man had worked at the elementary school, he had befriended Tad by letting him play with a football after classes, in the afternoon. Tad dropkicked it over and over, trying to get it through the uprights on the playground. One day, walking from school to his friend's house, as usual, an unusual thing happened. The man pulled alongside in a battered pickup, calling to him: "Need a ride, kid? Come on, get in."

Next thing he knew they were alone in the huge backyard of the grandmother's house, practicing moves -- blocking, end-running, "touch football." Then it began to drizzle, but the man urged him on. "Want to be good at it, or not? Practice, practice." Then Tad was playing center, hiking the football. The man shoved him down, pressed against him, pulled at his pants, got them opened and down, got Tad's underwear down, held him to the wet grass with strong arms, grunting, even giggling at times. The man was trying to put something in his behind.

Margie's cellar became a room of horror, with screams and cries. The man had tried to push into him, but the pain was so great Tad had struggled and flipped over, somehow, onto his back, even while in the madman's grip. "No!" he screamed. "Don't do that!" The sick smile had gleamed menacingly at him, then demands, then blows, but Tad refused to comply. Somewhere in his mind he knew what this was, someone had told him (a friend?) -- this was something to refuse, to escape, something bad, crazy.

He couldn't do any more, so Margie brought him upstairs, gave him water, told him to relax, to "leave it alone for now."

"He tried to rape me."

"Yes."

"He was from the school, yeah -- maintenance, or... janitor. I don't know. He said 'Call me Roy.' Yuck."

"Relax. Leave it alone. We'll get to it tomorrow, okay?"

"Okay," he said weakly, handing Margie the thirty-five
dollars.

Another client of hers came in the front door,
sheepishly. Tall, thin, older than Tad. They barely
glanced at each other when Tad made his way out, into the
sunshine, shocked, disoriented, worried. He remembered
more now -- hitting the crazy man with a rock -- but he'd
forgotten it all these years. What would tomorrow bring?

As a matter of fact, it took them four additional
sessions to completely reveal the entire episode, including
the aftermath, riding home with his mother who had picked
him up, as usual, at his friend's house across the street -
- an after-school routine, since Tad's school was near her
job, at the time. His brother went to another school.

The fifth therapy session was in essence a 'review,' a
rapid reliving of the whole nasty occurrence, from pickup
truck, on, to arriving at his home, a review to make sure
it truly happened, for Tad, and for Margie, to make sure
the entirety of it was "felt fully." As if it ever could
be.

"You'll need to do more, certainly, but this will do
for now. Take it easy. Go listen to some music."

As the madman had squeezed his throat, killing him,
Tad had clutched, miraculously, a rock from a broken-down
low wall within reach, a rock with plaster on it, or
cement, he didn't know which, a rock he felt compelled to
bang as hard as he could against the side of his attacker's
head, a blow which stunned the man, made him fall onto Tad,
nearly unconscious; but as Tad attempted to dislodge the
grip on his throat, to get away, the man revived enough to
retain that awful grip, at least with one powerful hand.
Yet, by then, their positions had reversed -- Tad above,
him below. Yet he couldn't get away. Quickly both hands
now squeezed his throat and all Tad could do was grab up
the rock and pound again and again at the man -- who
desperately tried to block the blows with one hand,
crushing Tad's throat with the other -- lucky for Tad. Had
he used both hands to protect himself the man would have
succeeded -- and killed Tad. Suddenly, due to the
sharpness of the rock's edge, and the force of Tad's
pounding, it penetrated the skull. Fluid, blood, sprang
out; Tad struck again. More blood, gushing, with a pinkish
substance, and the grip had lessened. Tad pulled free,
attempting to stand, dropped the rock, staggered backward,
fell -- his pants at his ankles. The man's eyes were half

opened, but he wasn't moving, one arm oddly poised upward, still. Tad was trembling, shaking, a reaction which overtook his body, uncontrollably, in the cellar with Margie. But not exactly "uncontrollably." He was allowing it. She urged him to release it all, to re-experience it all, to feel it all.

Yet, there was more; the worst, for Tad's future at that time, was yet to happen. He'd pulled up his pants, and staggered, choking, panting, the long way to the front yard of the house, to the street. It was getting dark; the drizzle was gone. He looked at his friend's house, he ran across the street, he tripped on the curb, he landed painfully on his hands. He saw the front door, ahead, he pushed himself up to stand and run to that door, but suddenly, the young Tad pictured his entrance, his terrified explanation to the other boy and his family inside. So he immediately stopped, crouched on the sidewalk, trembling wildly, hyperventilating, blood on his face and in his eyes. The police! He knew he'd killed someone, and he pictured himself telling them. On *PERRY MASON* reruns <u>they got you</u>, they didn't care what your excuse was, you were guilty of murder. On every TV program at the end, Tad had seen the killer was to be punished --

<u>executed</u>. He couldn't tell them inside the house -- he'd
be arrested, he'd be electrocuted.

That fateful erroneous moment turned the tide. Tad,
at barely twelve years old, knew what he had to do, and did
it, no matter how physically and psychologically wounded he
was. He returned to the grandmother's vast backyard. It
was nearly dark, now. He spied the body, unmoved,
unchanged, lying on the ground, eyes still half-open.

This was the last session with Margie. Young Tad had
buckled his pants by now, and knelt beside the body in the
grass. Blood soaked up into his jeans. The hole in the
man's head appeared small, but pinkish white gunk
protruded. Tad looked over the broken-down low wall, saw
trees, a wooded hillside sloping upward. He also saw wet
leaves, loose dirt, a "burial" ground. Using a piece of
slate from the crumbling wall, Tad got to the other side,
and dug. Dug and dug in the moist earth. To some avail;
just enough. He nearly passed out pushing the body over
the wall (really but a few stones high, only a foot high,
but as difficult a task as he'd ever performed, save,
perhaps, pounding the man with that rock), and into the
shallow grave. He covered it over with dirt and leaves. He
hid the rock there, too, after angrily striking the body in

the groin with it, in vengeance. He returned to the wet grass, and sat, sweating, audibly taking in as much air as his lungs could hold. Now what? He crept away, but saw the football where it had rolled. On his hands and knees Tad crawled to it, picked it up, stood shakily, flung it weakly into the bushes over the wall, over the grave, partway up the slope. He made it to the front yard, watching the street for cars. Where was the grandmother? Looking from a second-story window?

Tad slipped across the street into the house, bypassing the noisy TV room, barely answering "Yes" when someone asked if it was him, got into the nearest bathroom, washed his face (how it hurt!), wiped his shirt and pants with tissue, of the dark muddy blood, blew his nose, washed his hands over and over, drank handfuls of water from the faucet, and jumped in fear when his friend's mother knocked on the door asking, "Tad? Are you alright?"

"Yes," he croaked. "I'm alright."

Of course he wasn't. She was there when he emerged, after flushing the tissues down the toilet.

"What in the world happened?" Those were the last words he wanted to hear. She held up his face. "Oh my!"

She took him to the kitchen. His friend joined them, staring. She dabbed something (alcohol?), she applied an astonishingly painful red liquid ("Mercurochrome," Margie guessed), asking him again what had happened. He lied, a sudden outburst of foolishness, mingled with truth: "I fell on the sidewalk. I was running. I was late." That's all he could say.

She buttoned his shirt. "Were you in a fight?" The question scared him; he denied it, and to his great relief a smile turned up the corners of her mouth. "Oh no," she said, "of course not! You only fell on the sidewalk!"

Time gently lessened the devastating impact of these retrogressive revelations. Tad grew more comfortable with the "news." He'd killed a man (not as old as he'd seemed to 12-year-old Tad -- he had been, in fact, seen more accurately through Tad's twenty-three-year-old eyes, only perhaps twenty-one, or even less -- twenty). The realization, now, that he'd been afraid of being caught by the law, of being convicted of murder, stunned him. He'd suppressed that fear for all these years, had put it safely out of his conscious mind. "Emotional survival," Margie called it.

Asthma had set in after that event. Tad recalled this without the aid of therapy. He'd stayed home from school for two weeks. Now Tad understood: he'd been secretly afraid of the body being discovered, but as far as he knew, it wasn't. The grandmother, living alone, never noticed it beyond the wall, probably never ventured even into her backyard, never smelled it. The town was small, far outside of Los Angeles, the houses were far apart. The hills had coyotes. Maybe they'd carried "Roy" away, in pieces.

Tad told Zack, to Zack's surprise, who recommended a search of news reports after the approximate date of the remembered event. A good idea, but difficult to act on. Nevertheless, Tad researched in the library as much as he could -- scared, nervous, fretful. No report of a body, or even a missing man that fit the requirements. Three teenage boys had vanished about the same time, but their pictures, in the paper, proved inconclusive. It was hard to tell if one of them had been "Roy." Of course Tad could go back to the school to inquire, but fear prevented him taking that step. Although he now understood, mentally, as Margie and Zack assured him, that he had acted in self-defense, the fear of arrest remained. He couldn't talk himself out of it. It had haunted him inside, all these years, below the conscious level. It had obviously held him back, it had interfered with his life in many ways, as Margie explained. It had changed him from an extrovert to an introvert. No wonder he'd needed such pushing and prompting to go into acting. To do anything, really. He'd unconsciously been afraid of revealing too much about himself, of some smart police investigator finding out he wasn't the "sweet" boy he seemed, of checking his whereabouts on the evening of that old unsolved homicide he "kept working on."

And where was the pickup truck? Didn't Roy have a family who tried to find him? Sure, the police might know the answers to those questions, but Tad was unable to walk into the station to ask. The police might not feel the way Zack and Margie did.

But now he knew the source of his reluctance to engage in fights, at school, after that event. It wasn't only those bullies -- that may have led to some reluctance -- but this. No way he'd want to repeat that murder (but no, it wasn't a murder!). He'd thought, back then, that any fight might lead to a similar outcome: death, his or another's -- even after the memory had been suppressed.

Gradually, now, the fear of such an unlikely result diminished in the light of practical "analysis." At twelve he'd thought the potential great, but now, at twenty-three, he saw the chance of such a result (of a random fistfight) slim, or nonexistent. This insight was a reward of the therapy: conclusions drawn and "stuck" in one's mind, by a trauma, were dissolved when that trauma was "fully felt" in the present.

Maybe his acting would improve, because he'd be less withdrawn, more willing to express himself, not afraid a flash of emotion might cause suspicion -- "is he the guy who killed Roy?" -- and lead to his arrest. He <u>wasn't</u> guilty of murder. What he'd done was not something to be ashamed of -- unless you regarded hiding the body, keeping quiet, as shameful acts. But now Tad understood: his upbringing had been strict -- he'd learned to expect punishment for any accident, for knocking over a glass of milk at the dinner table, for breaking a tool in his father's garage. Harsh punishment, for a child, such as led Tad to conclude every move he made might produce parental disapproval. So of <u>course</u> a dead body would be disapproved of, regardless of the reason it came to be such, <u>at his hands</u>. Another child would have wept to the friends across the street, to his parents, even to the police, and been comforted, even congratulated, for courage. But not Tad. Not a child who had been punished severely for getting his shoes wet in the gutter, for slamming the screen door, for losing his jacket one day: sent to his room without dinner, spanked with a belt (by his mother), ignored cruelly (by his father), until the jacket was found in a neighbor's tree house -- at the age of seven -- and reminded often, usually at clothing stores, as a justification to not buy him a different jacket, later, that he wanted, getting instead a cheap one "because you'll only lose it." Tad had been "trained," as Margie explained, to dread extreme responses to normal childhood failings, that naturally a death he'd caused meant big trouble, in a twelve-year-old's reasoning.

He did more sessions in the basement -- finding pain in the "dog-taking" (at age eight), in painfully falling off his bike (at age fourteen), in being sent to his room so frequently for truly minor violations, etc. He also cried regarding the passing of his father, the report his dog was "put to sleep," the day his brother told him there was no Santa Claus, and called him a "weakling," punching Tad in the stomach. But Tad was running out of money, and, regardless of the evidence his attitude toward life was improving, stopped going in for therapy. He'd had enough. Naturally Margie disagreed, so he simply told her he'd renew the treatments when he had the money. But he never did.

The drag-racing movie left the theatres, Franklin called up with a series "regular" (continuous) role audition, which Tad considered but declined, reaffirming his decision to only do movies; one of the older actresses he'd dated called, inviting him to a party, and Sam brought over a white girl to spend the night. Tad agreed to stay out as late as he could (one a.m.), hanging over at Kiko's, eating, drinking, watching *THE LORD OF THE RINGS PART IV* (he didn't like it) and when Tad came into the bungalow he smelled marijuana, sprayed Ozium, slept on top of the covers, dreamed of being chased by gang members but escaping at the last minute into a distorted version of Universal Theme Park, woke up later than usual, drank coffee, showered (no sit-ups), drove to Malibu to park and sit on the beach with his shirt off, watching surfers, ate lunch at the Malibu Inn, left a message accepting the party invitation, drove to the market for food supplies, then to the bungalow, and took a nap. Sam was out. His phone ringing woke him up, but Tad didn't answer it. After more coffee he watched the news and listened to the message -- Faye, the actress, saying the party was postponed for a week, would that be okay? She was having trouble accommodating her guests' schedules. She called him "sweetheart.'

He thought about his therapy experiences, of the choking, of the blood, of his false fear of arrest, of his brother, of his father, of his dog. He called his mother, who, as always, didn't recognize his voice when he said hello.

"Yes?" she asked guardedly.

"It's me, Tad."

"Hi. How are you?"

"Fine. Just calling to see what's up."

"Oh, not anything. Where are you?"

"I'm in my apartment." Duh.

"Apartment? Don't you have a house?"

"Yes, right. You know what I mean."

"What's wrong?"

"Nothing's wrong. Why?"

"You sound angry."

"I'm not angry. Although I've been doing this regressive therapy. It recalls painful times from the past, so <u>sometimes</u> you are angry. But not now."

"Regressive therapy?"

"Yes. It's great. You should try it. Like Primal Therapy."

"Oh. No, I don't like that."

"What do you know about it?" he asked, wishing he hadn't.

"Primal Therapy? I read the book."

"And?"

"I didn't like it. I suppose you're mad at me now for all the bad mother things you believe I did."

"What? Like what?"

"You tell me."

"What?" he asked again.

"Don't you see it that way?"

"Not really. You tried."

"Don't you think I was a bad mother?"

"No," he lied. "The therapy isn't like that -- it doesn't make you draw judgments." Another lie.

"Really?"

"Well, kind of, but you let go of things. It doesn't stay inside you."

"Do you scream?"

"Yes.

"It's dangerous, isn't it?"

"No," he said, regretting telling her about it.

"How can you know you're not making it up? Making up these past things?"

"You -- you just know it. It's real." He wanted to tell her about Roy, but didn't. She wouldn't believe him anyway. "Like, when Dad died, I never felt the grief enough. I did it, though. In this therapy stuff."

"Grief? Now? You were very upset at the time, weren't you?"

"I know, but I shut it off. I never felt all of it. You must have painful events you never felt all the way. You should try it. It's very freeing."

"Very what?"

"Free-ing. I feel better, a lot better."

"Did you go to a hospital, or what?"

"I -- yeah," he lied. "A clinic." He didn't want to explain about Margie's cellar, knowing his mother would criticize that as being of doubtful value, even though she didn't believe in the treatment anyway.

"Did you pay for it?"

"Sure I did."

"How much did you pay?"

"It doesn't matter. It was worth it."

"Well, when are you coming up to visit?"

"Pretty soon. I can't get away now. No jobs at present, so I have to stretch my money."

"No? What about that agent?"

"Just not any jobs. I don't know why."

"I told you," she said simply.

The pain release therapy had galvanized him to approach life differently, to express himself more openly. First off, Tad explained once more to Franklin his hopes of finding a work of art, and his desire to wait for it. Franklin begrudgingly reiterated comprehension, if not enthusiasm. Second, he applied for unemployment insurance, and received it. Third, he left a message for Amanda, thanking her for introducing him to Margie, and for being his friend generally. He saw there was virtue in expressing feelings, not danger, not arrest, not punishment.

He was less shy, although still affected by the tendency. He encouraged Sam to try the therapy, but to no avail. Sam demurred, insisting he wasn't a "psycho." Tad accepted it. Who was he to push anyone into it? He burned a candle, he listened to more music, he allowed the revelations ("connections," Margie called them) to filter up in his consciousness. For example, Tad didn't have to be afraid of his older brother anymore -- they were of comparable physical size, not like when they were young. Arthur would be hard-pressed to get away with punching Tad in the stomach now, duh!

"Hi, I'm Gidget," the short 40ish woman in the doorway said. "You Tad?"

"Yes, hi."

"Come in, come in!" She put her hand under his arm and pulled him into the house. Tad saw people standing in the living room, heard music, saw an opened patio doorway, more people on the deck, outside, and felt a kiss on his cheek. It was Faye, in a bikini.

"Hi, lover." Her eyes were glassy. "You're here!" She smiled at Gidget. "Will you show him around? I have to watch the taco meat." But she stopped as she turned away. "You aren't a vegetarian, are you?"

"No," he said.

"I made meatless chili, too. And chicken. And -- just take him, Gidget." She fled to the kitchen next to the front room. There was a staircase that led up to another floor, photos mounted on the walls, loaded bookcases. Her furnishings were expensive, not beach-style. A few faces turned his way as Gidget pulled him further inside, leaving the front door open. She wore a bikini, also, underneath her white robe, white sandals, and a tattoo near her ankle.

"This is Tad Walsh, everybody. He worked with Faye in *CAPITAL...*" She looked at him. "What was it?"

"*CAPITAL GAME.*"

She laughed and said "I can never remember that! He was a crooked card shark, right?"

"One of them. Faye was our leader." The faces waited expectantly. A moment of social dread gripped him, but it faded, so he added, "We cheated some politicians and they, they sent a bunch of thugs to kick us out of town, and, uh, my character defends Faye -- but, I don't want to tell you the end."

"No, don't tell us the end," a pretty woman in a blue dress promptly declared. "It sounds intriguing."

"Very intriguing," another guest agreed, holding out his hand to Tad. "I'm Mickey Brown. Nice to meet you." He wore a shirt and tie under a yellow sweater, and white pants.

They shook, Tad responding, "Thanks. Glad to meet you." Mickey smiled sweetly.

"Joan McKay," the pretty woman said, offering her hand. Tad shook two more hands and heard two more names, but lost track. Gidget said, "Come on, Tad, I'll show you the deck. Excuse us."

They walked out onto the large wooden patio, making their way through other partygoers to the railing. Surf splashed in the dark, although the sand directly below was illuminated by a light under the deck. Gidget held onto Tad's arm and asked, "How do you like it?"

"Beautiful." Wondering what to say, he asked, "Have you been swimming?"

"No! I was getting a tan, though, earlier. I came earlier to help Faye," she laughed. "Sort of. But she has it all under control. Except for Barnell."

"Who?"

"Barnell Benjamin, Faye's -- what should I say? Off-and-on boyfriend? Don't you know him?" Tad shook his head. "Well, that's your good fortune. He's here, getting pie-eyed." She turned to look back into the house. "Don't see him. Perhaps he's sitting down. Come on, do you want to meet Sidney Parks?"

"Sure." They moved into the center of the deck and Gidget touched a 60ish woman's arm. "Sidney? Pardon me." Sidney turned, smiling, caught Tad's eye, and Gidget introduced them. Sidney's dress looked expensive, to Tad, and a diamond ring on her left hand sparkled.

"He worked with Faye in, uh --"

"*CAPITAL GAME*. It isn't out yet. How are you?"

"Good." She looked him over appraisingly. "An actor, then?"

"Yes. Kind of."

"Kind of?" She laughed.

"He's an actor," Gidget affirmed. "Going to write about him?"

"Maybe I will. Have you any secrets, Tad?"

"No, I -- no. Are you a writer?"

"Is she a writer!" Gidget exclaimed.

"I'm sorry," he said.

"She's famous. A famous novelist. Sidney's books worry people, they don't know if she's writing about them. We always try to figure out who she's really --"

"Don't pay any attention to that," Sidney interposed. "I make everything up."

"Oh heck, yes," Gidget said.

Tad laughed. "You can write about me. I'm just starting out, though. I was lucky to get in a movie with Faye."

"And take her on a date," Gidget added.

"Oh, how did it go?" Sidney asked. "But wait a second." She turned to her companion, a 50ish man in a robe and swimsuit. "This is Charles. This is Tad."

They said hello, and Gidget ran to get Tad a drink, and the evening hastened forward, Tad sitting to eat with Charles and Sidney, telling about his date with Faye, about the movie, hearing Sidney's recital of Charles' accomplishments (producing movies for a major studio), of Charles' desire to see *CAPITAL GAME*, then Tad relating his background, and Sidney's hope of seeing him again, asking again if Tad knew any secrets, etc., etc. Faye, now dressed, had joined them at last, at their table, and complained Barnell was drunk, refusing to leave, but was Tad enjoying himself?

Barnell finally caused a ruckus, approaching their table and denouncing Tad as Faye's latest "conquest," Tad rising to defend her, Barnell demanding he and Tad settle it "outside."

"On the beach?" Tad asked.

Mickey interceded forcefully, taking the "off-and-on boyfriend" out to the front, returning shortly to report that a cab had been summoned, and that Barnell was sorry.

Faye was suddenly in tears, and many of her guests delicately departed, expressing sympathy, Gidget, now intoxicated herself, cursing at Barnell as he staggered to his cab, Tad suffering extreme embarrassment, but sitting beside Faye honorably, dismissing her repeated apologies. Sidney joked, "If only you had gone out on the beach with him!" Charles reprimanding her, Sidney glaring at him, Faye holding Tad's hand, the housekeepers clearing away dishes, other guests leaving, Faye standing to receive kisses, and Mickey patting Tad on the back, after they sat down again, Tad thanking him for his assistance, a tall black actor named Roland saying, "I tend to agree with Sidney, there," Tad laughing, saying, "You remind me of my roommate," a silence following, Sidney asking, "A <u>male</u> roommate?" Tad explaining, "No, no, it's not like <u>that</u>. I mean, he just likes to fight," Mickey glaring at Tad, and Gidget warning, "Be careful, you'll hurt his feelings," indicating Mickey, Tad standing, confused, apologetic, Roland laughing, Tad saying "Look, I'm sorry. I don't mean there's anything wrong with it. It's just not the way I..." being unable to complete his sentence, Gidget laughing now, and Faye, too, and Mickey, feigning bruised feelings, replying, "After all I've done for you!"

So the party was, in fact, a success. Tad slept over. But strangely Faye asked him to stay in the guest bedroom. She wouldn't say why, only begged him to understand, and not to leave.

Tad didn't sleep well, partly from thinking Barnell would show up, partly from thinking how the therapy had helped free him of shyness, of the fear of physical confrontation, and how the whole evening proved it. He listened to the waves hitting the sand, thought about Faye in the next room, pondered his future, and thrilled at the awareness he was spending the night in Malibu.

Two of the crook-role films Tad had done went straight to DVD and sat on the shelves, amidst other seemingly countless films, unwatched, he feared. He did purchase a copy of *MAD SCIENTIST*, took it to the hospital, and gave it to Francine's father, who seemed happy, but, yet, wistfully sad during the bedside visit. Tad asked him if he got to go outside, which he said he did, and asked how Francine was doing, but her father didn't seem to have any information, or perhaps, couldn't remember. He told Tad he'd been shot in the back of his head (during the first Gulf War). Once again Tad thanked him for his service and promised to return for a visit when he could.

After leaving, the ridiculous guilt struck him hard, made him feel dizzy, made him drink too much that evening. Why did he feel so guilty? Because men and women had made sacrifices? And Tad hadn't? He resolved to do something for his country, but couldn't imagine what that would be. Volunteer? He didn't believe in the war, now. He didn't want to go to Iraq. He could go to Afghanistan, certainly.

Well, not certainly. They might send him anywhere. No guarantees. It was frustrating not to know what to do.

In the morning Tad concluded he could one way or the other be in a movie which would promote democracy, but how to get in one? He left a message for his agent haltingly, ineptly making the request: could Franklin look for a part which affirmed American values? A film that honored our soldiers? That might do it.

While Tad waited, he used part of the money he'd been making to get an overdue, complete, physical examination. (The basic doctor checkups for movie production insurance purposes were not enough, everyone told him.) Still, slyly accompanying his half-day doctor's visit testing was the inevitable (for him) heightened sense of mortality, which slyly nagged at him until all the results were in, many days thereafter -- a clean bill of health, no sign of asthma, nothing wrong, in fact, aside from a corn on his right foot that required treatment. Safe, he thought, for now. The dread of early death passed.

He asked Sam if he felt that nagging fear regarding physical exams -- Sam said "Hell, no. But I sure don't like that prostate test!"

For a week or two Tad added push-ups to his morning exercise, but a pain in his shoulder caused him to drop that, for now. Instead he did more arm-circles at the track before his run.

One morning Kiko suggested they go to the gym with Sam, someday, but Tad replied, "I tried weights in college. Not my thing."

"There's other things you can do there, man." They were loosening up at the track.

"I know, but I don't want to. Can't explain it." Tad did a few knee-bends, jogged in place in preparation for the run, and Kiko did the same, remarking, "Don't you know women like muscles?"

During the late 1960's Mr. Christian had gone to U.C. Berkeley ("and stayed there," he liked to joke), studying Theatre Arts and protesting the war in Vietnam, becoming a Conscientious Objector and avoiding the draft in Canada. He got the drama department job at Fullerton High in the 1970's, and when Tad's family moved to the area in the 1990's, was trying to push his students to "dig deep," to find the "reality" of the characters they created in class and in the senior plays, and urged a number of his best students to give the profession a shot. Nothing ventured, nothing gained, Mr. Christian felt.

He was a believer in all acting students reading classic novels to see what human beings went through, to aid in an understanding of human behavior (so essential to role-creating on stage). One of the old books he advised Tad to study was *FROM HERE TO ETERNITY*, and after reading it to then see the classic movie, to watch the fine work by Monty Clift and Burt Lancaster. And the women's roles too, to see what real acting was all about.

But no such powerful soldier film came Tad's way, in Hollywood. Those good old days were way over, he told Mr. Christian. He waited and hoped, of course, for his agent to miraculously find a film with a *FROM HERE TO ETERNITY* message. Waiting and hoping and studying to find good parts was the common Hollywood effort (trial, actually), common to bit player and major star and just about everyone in between. When Julia Roberts got *ERIN BROCKOVICH*, "the angels were on her side," Mr. Christian told him, and wished for Tad the equivalency in a male role. So Tad hung in there, comforted by the support, loving Mr. Christian as a father and a mentor, suffering, biding his time, residing in the dark, vexing jail-cell of "thespian" unemployment.

Occasionally Tad thought of Francine (wasn't she eighteen by now?) and pledged to seek her out, soon, but didn't. She'd have a boyfriend, now, and would not be interested in an unemployed half-crazed former one-time lover. Then again, how did he know? A feeling of inadequacy engulfed him. But Tad vowed to call her, or drive to her mother's house if the number was disconnected. Hadn't he promised Francine he would? At the least he could find out how she was doing. What was holding him back?

His inaction irked him, pained him, forced him to puzzle out the reason. All Tad came up with was a fear she wouldn't like him anymore, wouldn't be interested. So one day, alone in the bungalow, he locked the doors and shut the windows and turned up the stereo and "drew" out the emotion, a pillow against his face, in bed, feeling, feeling, seeing himself in first one, then two unpleasant encounters with girls in middle school, avoiding eye contact, feebly joking, being rejected, hurting, now crying, in his bungalow, yelling in agony, knowing he'd struck out because the specter of Roy's body, dead, underground beyond that wall, deprived Tad of the capacity to reach out, to engage a female for fear she'd notice he was "aggressive," that he liked girls, that it was an "indication," a clue that <u>he would have fought</u>, and killed Roy, that the police would <u>know</u> he was the one who'd done it, and hidden it, and then he'd be arrested, and taken to prison, and executed. All this in his thirteen-fourteen-year-old mind, secretly interfering with his attempts to express himself to, and bond with, girls. They'd know! They'd know he killed him because he liked women! How strange, how dumb, how illogical yet perfectly logical once he felt the pain, the deep pain, and could see the truth.

So Tad called Francine's number (it was changed), he drove to her mother's house, he reached her finally, they had lunch at Carrows, they talked. Yes, she had a boyfriend, yes, she was glad he'd contacted her, no, she didn't think they should date for now, no, she didn't harbor any resentment from the past, yes, she had seen some of his movies, yes, she still wanted to be an actress, no, she wasn't ready to get an agent, yes, her father was doing okay, yes, she was glad they'd gotten together back then, and boy was she sorry for her behavior (partly) because he could have gotten into a "whole lot of trouble."

After the private screening of *ROUGH KIDS* (the movie where Tad had climbed a fence), the director hugged Destiny, raving excessively as to her performance, and invited her out for a drink.

"Some other time," she said, living up to her reputation as 'distant.' "I'm busy."

"One tiny bitty small drink!"

"It appears you've already had that drink, Gregory." She didn't bother to laugh. "Some other time." She walked away gritting her teeth. They always thought they could nail her. Why? She never led them on -- they must think all actresses are whores.

"See you. Thank you. It's wonderful," she told the producer and his wife, who had held the private screening at their home in Beverly Hills.

"You're terrific," the producer said, jumping from his chair, but Destiny was out the door, briskly escaping to her car. She was "busy" that night. Her boyfriend Steve intended to show her his latest find, a "lovely" penthouse condo in West Hollywood. This was a ritual she tolerated -- he was endlessly discovering a potential home for them, if she'd ever say yes to marriage. But that was very unlikely. Steve was an engaging man, true, but Destiny wanted more -- more income, more status, more acclaim. Any day she might land a part with an eligible star, and the rest would be history, so to speak.

Unfortunately for her plans, a hard fact of life would doom them to virtual futility -- any eligible star would love her, and move on, content to remain "eligible," content to seek the path of least resistance, the constant advent of new relationships. Destiny would lower her sights as she hit thirty, and marry a non-star actor or producer or studio executive or powerful agent, settling for that, rather than single life. Along the way she'd have closed the door on true love, on greater happiness. Unless she was triumphantly lucky. And that luck would have to extend to finding a movie star who could be faithful. Possible, of course. But if he was unmarried and rich and popular, not too likely, and, even less likely to propose.

She called Steve from her car to alert him she was on her way, and would meet him, shortly, in front of his office. But there was no answer, so she left a message: "You told me you'd be there. Where are you?"

She parked and waited at his building. The parking lot was nearly empty, which made Destiny uneasy.

He arrived in his own car ten minutes later, just as she was at the point of leaving. When he pulled up, got out, and walked to her window to say hello, she replied with: "What happened?"

The deal was off, he told her. We need to talk, he told her. Stop yelling at me, he told her, come up to my office.

Noting Steve's uncharacteristic manner, Destiny surrendered to his request. In the empty public relations company offices, in the waiting room, seated in a cozy client's chair, Destiny listened. His candor didn't impress her. She left after ten minutes, went to her car, drove away, her face flushed, her breathing unsteady. She phoned her one good friend, Hilda.

"Steve broke up with me! He found someone else. Please, can I come over there?"

Meanwhile, at the producer's home, the director Gregory had remained, basking in the praise (overdone) lavished on him by the screenwriter and her husband and a handful of guests who quickly departed. Gregory had his "tiny bitty" drink there (indeed not his first of the evening), congratulating his hosts on a "superb" night, a "super" movie. Eliot and Joy Greenfield planned another youth film, wanted Gregory and the writer Penny to create it, wanted Destiny "for sure" to be in it, and although her part as a policeman's wife in *ROUGH KIDS* hadn't been large, hoped she'd take the lead. "I can talk her into it," boasted Gregory. "I'll make her take it!" The booze was talking, but the Greenfields had no doubt that that would be the case. Their new project needed a solid actress, which Destiny certainly was, and they could satisfy the investors with a big name in the male lead opposite her.

"Joy and I will produce this one together," Eliot announced proudly. Joy had had only marginal involvement with *ROUGH KIDS*, and her name was not in the credits. "It's her idea. A love story, a car chase, a romantic road movie. I trust her instincts." He patted Joy's arm. "You meet with her, Penny. Write up an outline."

"Terrific," Penny responded, wondering how much they'd pay. Surely more than this last one. But that discussion should come later. If they liked her rough draft, she'd ask for double her price. Why not? "What's the male lead? A Mel Gibson type? Action and sexual appeal?"

"Exactly," Eliot answered, and glanced at his wife. "Along those lines? What do you think?"

"Um-huh. But younger."

"That's right," he said.

"I personally found the mechanic interesting. What's his name?" Joy asked.

"The mechanic? Tad Walsh," Eliot answered. "Yes, yes. But not for the lead, surely."

"No, no, only, somewhere. Right, Gregory? How do you feel about him? Okay to work with?"

"Very nice," the director conceded. "Introverted, really, but always did what I wanted."

"We can make a part for him somewhere. I liked him," Joy said. "A hitchhiker, or... I don't know. Along the road, when they're running away."

Tad turned twenty-four, succumbing to his mother's pressure to spend the weekend at her house in Portland. Of course she didn't pay the air fare, but did feed him and give him a few birthday presents. That was the good part. The bad part was having a big argument, about what, it was not clear. They disagreed on so many issues, it all congealed into a soup of unpleasant contention. Mainly she tried to make him admit he didn't like her, which he refused to do. Frankly, he wasn't sure himself. He didn't hate her, he didn't love her. In the middle a cross-current of emotions churned hot and cold. The more she pushed him, however, the more he disliked her. When her two women friends made a pitch, out of nowhere, in defense of her, Tad disengaged further. She'd obviously overstated (lied), and asked them (privately) to sling a counteroffensive of "voluntary" advocacy on her behalf. Naturally it made him feel bad, but didn't change his mind. They said:

"She's such a wonderful person," and "Maybe you're too hard on her."

What had she told them? More pretense, more distortions, more falsehood.

"She's okay in our book," they said.

He bit his tongue, figuratively. Now could he convince them she was a liar? And why should he? The three women had been visiting in another room of the house, and when the two friends came out, past Tad, who was sitting in the kitchen, they included those comments in their goodbyes. His mother had sent them, of course, while remaining in the other room. After they left she came out to resume the argument: "Well?"

"Nice try," he told her.

"What are you talking about?"

"Getting them to attack me."

"Attack you? What happened?"

"As if you don't know. To plead your case."

"Well?"

"Stop pretending. I know you. How many times have you used <u>me</u> as your agent? Or Arthur? It's an old ploy. Like the time I talked about that diet book, and you said: 'I wish you'd tell Randy about it. He could do to lose weight. But <u>please</u> don't tell him I asked you to.' Remember?"

"Randy <u>needed</u> to lose weight. When you talked about that diet --"

"That isn't the point. You used me, as if him losing weight was <u>my</u> idea. You do that all the time."

"That's ridiculous."

"One time I heard you on the phone telling Arthur to come over, 'to cheer up Tad.' Direct quote. I wasn't unhappy then. You only said that to make him --" Her steely eyes caused Tad to stop.

"What? Make him what?"

"You got him to think I was sad so he'd come over. It was a <u>lie</u>."

"That was a long time ago."

"So what? It's your typical way of tricking people to get what you want."

"What was I supposed to have wanted, may I ask?"

"You wanted him to come here, pretending he wasn't on an errand of yours, to make you look good because we were arguing, to make me lose the argument, that's what."

"To make me look good? How?"

"Oh, boy. By him thinking I was in a bad mood, so there wasn't anything wrong with you, that -- I don't know. Something. You tell me."

"Impossible."

"Of course! Because it makes you look conniving. We can't have that now, can we?"

"That's absurd. Maybe I did say it to him, but you're exaggerating. That hurts."

He returned to Los Angeles frustrated and discouraged. She'd never change. It was up to Tad to be healthy, mentally, to keep away from her, to maybe go see Margie for more sessions. But he finally realized his mother's goal, while riding in the taxicab from the airport. It was all in a book he'd read, about possessive mothers. She wanted him only for herself, like a "lover," the author had observed, in reference to a particular narcissistic "type." All for themselves, no matter what the scheme to bring it about, no matter what the trick. Disparage Tad, his life and choices, so he'd feel he needed her above all else. The final move to win victory, the author wrote, was to play the "jilted lover," a tactic Tad now recognized. When he got to his bungalow he at last felt relieved, safe, refreshed, not vulnerable to her subtle implications, her endless ploys.

One of his recovered memories had been her repeated toying with his penis, in his early youth -- two, three, four years old. Tad hadn't mentioned that to Margie. Now he knew his mother was sick, was always drawn to him as a sexual plaything -- her "favorite," she'd said, more than once, even to Arthur. Yeah, favorite <u>plaything</u>. She may not actually want to have sex with him, but she <u>almost</u> wanted it. Why would she tell him of her bedroom behavior with his father? Why would she mention her "pubic hairs" to him? That had occurred during a previous visit, in connection to questions and comments her old boyfriend Randy had made to Tad, back in the nineties, asking Tad if he'd ever slept in a bed with his mother (which he had, many years ago, one or two times -- don't all boys?) and had Tad "seen" anything? Off guard, Tad lied "yes," to please the boyfriend (the pattern again of not angering anyone, not creating a violent reaction which might lead to death). The boyfriend had later told his mother, who suddenly, <u>years</u> later, referred to the comment.

"Was it my pubic hairs? That's it, isn't it? Don't be ashamed. I don't mind. You were excited?"

At the time it had badly distressed him, without Tad understanding why. Now he knew why. She'd been encouraging it -- <u>not discouraging it</u>, like a normal mother would have. And it wasn't even true, he hadn't seen anything!

He drank a beer and watched television after unpacking, resolving firmly: no more birthday junkets, no more Christmastime gatherings. By midnight Sam came in, tired from work. Everyone had an acting job except Tad, it seemed. Probably Francine was even doing another play. He'd call Franklin tomorrow.

But when he did, Franklin's calm response was, "It's pretty slow at the moment. Don't lose faith. I'm doing as you said, looking for a special part."

"Thanks."

"Anytime you change your mind and want to go up for a series regular, let me know." Franklin couldn't control the sarcasm in his voice. "It happens, though, we've missed this year's pilot season, minus a few exceptions."

"Well, that movie with Destiny is coming out. That'll help."

"Definitely that will help. In the meantime I'm hunting through the breakdowns."

"Thanks," he repeated. "Well, I'll talk to you later."

"Um-huh. Goodbye."

He hung up and called Faye; she didn't answer, so he left a message.

"It's Tad. I'm wondering how you've been doing. I'm fine. Uh, say, I was thinking, how's about we stay in the same room the next time?" He chuckled a bit and hung up. Was that bold enough? Then he called Hal, who did answer, so they argued about domestic spying, the war in Iraq, and global warming.

Meanwhile, although Tad knew nothing of the Greenfields' planned project, his mood was upbeat regarding *ROUGH KIDS*, and his own minor, burgeoning notoriety.

It seemed a natural result of having his movies come out in theatres, but nonetheless a gratifying one, when people at markets, or waitresses at counters, occasionally stared fixedly at him, and said he looked familiar, and recognized him from *MASTERMIND* or *BURNING RUBBER*, or something else, and even asked for his autograph. Once Arthur even called to congratulate him on his performance in *CAPITAL GAME*, on DVD. These moments happened infrequently, but often enough, now, to generate an inner satisfaction he never felt before in his life.

Tad kept collecting unemployment, waiting for the big role. Kiko got a part in a cable movie, which filmed in Arizona, and when he returned informed Tad he'd fallen in love with the script supervisor -- a girl from Utah who wanted to get married.

"She's not a Mormon," Kiko told him, "so it's okay for her to marry an Asian. But my folks will object. She's white as milk."

"So what?"

"I'm supposed to marry another Korean, or Thai girl, since my grandfather was from Thailand."

"Will you give in?"

They were in Kiko's apartment after a run at the track. Kiko sat on his hands on his couch. Tad was in a small chair by the window, drinking water. Traffic noise filtered in, filling the conversational pause.

"No, I like her too much. But it'll cost me."

"What do you mean?" Tad asked.

"My folks have property. A house all arranged as a wedding gift -- but not now. Not anymore. No way, José."

"If you love her what does a house matter? You can get your own someday."

Kiko shrugged and reached for his bottle of water on the coffee table, took a gulp, and shook his head. "Negatory, dude. I'll be an old man by that time. We'll have to live in this dump."

"So? Don't be a fool. Take a chance, marry her."

Kiko only looked at Tad, without nodding.

Amanda phoned to talk about life -- hers. And Tad's therapy.

"You want to have breakfast tomorrow?" she asked.

"Okay. Be glad to. Where?"

"I don't know."

"Uh... Carrows?"

"Aren't you tired of that place? How about Abe's Deli? You know?"

"Sure, fine. I remember where it is. What time?"

"Eleven?"

"Okay," Tad responded.

"Margie said you did great."

"Seemed like it. Have you done any more?"

"Oh yeah. Incredible. I feel good."

"Right on. Big stuff?"

"Not like you. She told me a little."

"Good. I'm not -- it's not a secret. I still feel funny about it, though. Afraid I'll get caught, even though I know I did what I had to do."

"Well, there's one thing you can do. Margie said to suggest it."

"What?" He didn't care they'd been discussing his killing the guy -- a good sign, for him. It showed he was more accepting of the whole travail. Only it was very unprofessional of Margie.

"She said if you went to the police and told them what happened, and saw they didn't care to prosecute -- which they wouldn't -- it'd help you realize how, you know, there's nothing to be afraid of."

"Not sure I can do that."

"No?"

"She already mentioned that, I think. Or maybe I thought of it myself. Still... it's... look, it worries me. Like, would my version be believed? It's only my word."

"Of course," Amanda replied. "You can't see that because you still feel guilty. They'd give you a medal, really. He'd probably done it before, maybe killed boys before you!"

"I know."

"Just think it over."

"I'm sure you're right, I'm sure Margie's right. Doing it, that's not easy. And who would I ask?"

"I don't know," she said. Call the Homicide Department."

"Oh God."

"Sorry. Let's talk tomorrow."

"Okay." They hung up, Tad knowing in his heart that it was good advice. But could he do it?

Abe's was a nice little deli -- tables like any coffee shop, but closer together, a grocery-style takeout section near the front with food offerings behind glass, for those in a hurry, a young hostess, older waitresses, good items on the menu. Tad preferred Carrows -- more room -- but this was Amanda's choice, and he wasn't complaining. There was even counter seating, which he'd forgotten about. After they ordered she launched into her own therapy discoveries -- painful early teasing about her breasts, the rapes at the high school parties, an aunt who called her "ugly." All of these traumas were not, in fact, discoveries, since she already remembered them, but the pain in each case had been suppressed, had not been "fully felt." After screaming and crying at Margie's, the release resulted in contentment, the shame abated, the inner assent (to her aunt's claims) became healthy dissent.

"I'm not ugly," she told him.

"Absolutely not," he agreed.

"__And__, listen, even if I were, conventionally speaking, my aunt would still be wrong, because she meant, really, there was no hope for me, which is just stupid. I see that now. Looks aren't everything. Far from it. My aunt's the one with the problem."

"Right." Their breakfast had arrived, but neither was eating, for some reason.

"Eat," Amanda said. "Don't wait. I'm excited, I can't start yet."

"Yeah. It's incredible, isn't it? How we carry these mistaken ideas around?"

"Eat."

He did, while Amanda smiled at him, and said, "I want to thank you for letting me stay with you. And for being so kind to me."

"Kind? Okay."

"You were. And I'm sorry I ran away."

"You didn't run away."

"No, really. I did. But I couldn't help it."

"Afraid? Of intimacy?"

"Yes," she answered. "You guessed it."

"Eat," he told her.

She did. Tad wondered if she'd ask to resume their relationship, but by the end of the meal she hadn't, so he abandoned the idea.

He spoke of his discoveries, of his fear of going to the police, of his knowledge it would be good to do, of his willingness, at least, to consider the suggestion.

"Guess I need to work at it some more. But... are you going to keep at it? I'm kind of worn out, or --"

"Yes, I'm going to. Don't worry. When you feel up to it you can call her." Amanda held his hand at the table, and looked into his eyes. The busboy took away their plates.

"We're just friends?" Tad asked.

"Friends," she replied.

"It's hard for me to trust a woman, I'm finding out."

"And for me, to trust a man," she laughed.

In the parking lot at her car Amanda appeared pensive, mumbling a couple of indistinct words and then telling him, "I have a secret I want to reveal. After our movie I received two -- or three, I don't remember -- offers, to be in more movies to show my breasts, but, heck, I couldn't do that. I turned 'em down!"

The Democrats had swept into control, in both the House and the Senate. Tad was disappointed with the announcement they wouldn't try to impeach Bush over the Iraq invasion lies.

"What a bunch of kiss-asses," he complained to Hal, on the phone.

"Man, take it easy. I know how you feel, but it's a waste of time."

"What is?"

"Trying to impeach him. Don't tell me you think he committed a crime."

"Maybe he did," Tad responded.

"A 'high' crime?"

"Yeah, maybe. They can hold a hearing, can't they? Check into it?"

"Tad, don't get mad, but Congress knows he didn't do anything that bad. Impeachment hearings would backfire."

"Bullshit. Just look into it, why won't they? I'll tell you why -- they're afraid of him."

"Well, they could be afraid of something. I'm guessing it's a lot to do about nothing, and they all know it."

"Stop going in circles! An investigation would show us if there's anything to it, or if, maybe, you're right about something for a change!" Hal hung up on him.

Destiny sent two e-mails when she found out the producers wanted her in their next film, one to her father and one to Hilda. She didn't feel like speaking with either of them on the phone. Her father constantly whined about his furniture business ("this damn economy") and Hilda would ask if she was dating anyone ("don't sit on your ass watching TV").

All Destiny wanted to do was brag. She was thrilled Eliot and Joy were having the script tailored to her -- that was a giant step in the right direction. But Gregory posed a problem. She'd have to fight him off the entire time. But it was worth it if they got a "big name" for the part opposite her. Who would it be? George Clooney? No, he must be fifty. Christian Bale? Russell Crowe?

It didn't matter, except Destiny wanted a "single" actor. But this may not be the time. It was, after all, a low-budget deal, like *ROUGH KIDS*. All she wanted was a success! Then good parts would roll in like manna from heaven.

Franklin's other two clients, aside from Destiny, Zack, and Tad, were not working at all. Both were talented, versatile, and unemployable, "for some reason."

After initial success, as a comedy team in a short-lived series, Michelle and Lucille demanded too much money (regardless of Franklin's pleas to the contrary) and most producers shunned them. And the rumor they were gay was certainly not helpful. As advanced and sophisticated as Hollywood seemed to the rest of the world, lesbians had a hard time finding work there.

Which is why the new script for Destiny's love story made Franklin sit up straight in his chair. He'd been reading, late, at the office, his mind wandering. Destiny had told him she wanted his opinion, but Franklin had to read the script, regardless, because Joy fervently inquired about Tad for the hitchhiker role, and anyway, an agent <u>ought</u> to read (at least superficially) whatever material is sent respecting his or her clients.

PAIR OF ACES showed promise for the first fifteen pages: the drug deal gone bad, the shootout, the male lead barely escaping. But then, absurdly, he takes a waitress with him, on the road. Destiny will ask haughtily: "Why would I join him in his escape? The waitress is too silly." And, that flaw aside, the mad drive to Arizona is fraught with implausibility: the pursuing drug dealers are caricatures -- inept, gruesome idiots. And then the two fall in love in a motel room, complete with naked shower scene. Destiny will hate it.

But, after their car crashes, two women drive them in an SUV across the state line. Two funny women. Two zany women. Two bonded, friendly, idiosyncratic women -- perfect for Michelle and Lucille.

Franklin flipped the pages forward to see what happened. The women drive to their home in Sedona and give their SUV to the lovers to "Carry on! You two are so cute together!" Implausible, but doable. He immediately phoned Joy's office, leaving a message regarding his two "wonderful" clients. "Would you consider them? I'll send headshots over in the morning."

Franklin closed the script and left his office, swearing to finish it at his leisure, later. Tad's role could wait. Destiny's objections could wait. He was too excited to think of all that.

Joy brought Michelle and Lucille in for a meeting with Gregory, and they were hired on the spot. Sometimes it worked that way.

Meanwhile Faye had a cold and was hanging around her house, taking aspirin, drinking extra water, complaining to her friend Rea, on the phone, how achy she felt. Another

call came in, so she told Rea goodbye, and coughed, and

answered it. Mickey.

"Hi, sweetie. Can I do anything for you?" He already

knew she was sick.

"No, Mickey. I'll survive."

"You call Tad?"

"No. Why?"

"Wondering. How's he doing?"

"Gosh, I -- haven't spoken with him in weeks. Should

I?"

"I would."

She laughed and coughed again. "Honey, are you

jealous? Want me to give you his phone number?"

"Me steal from you?" Mickey quipped. "How lurid. No,

call him, ask him to bring chicken soup. Get comforting."

She laughed and coughed again. "Stop!"

"Just call him. I'll drop over, if you want. Can you

eat anything?"

"No. I don't know. I should, huh?"

"Give me his number, I'll do it."

"Thanks, Mickey, but that boy's not interested in me.

I'm old."

"You're only forty!"

"If you say so."

"Or is it forty-one?" Mickey asked nonchalantly.

"Whatever. Call him."

"Alright. And yes, do come over. When?"

"After six. Okay?"

"Okay," Faye said. "See you, darling."

She called Tad, but didn't invite him over, not caring to spread germs, and fearing he'd say no. But Tad promised to call her in a few days, "When you're feeling better. I'd like to see you. Seems like a hundred years since your little party. Which reminds me -- no more trouble from whatever his name is, the drunk guy?"

"No."

"Good." There was an awkward silence until Tad added: "Get well. I really want to see you again. I'll call in a few days. Or do you need a week?"

"Who knows? I don't feel that terrible."

"Well, yeah, that's the spirit. Get some rest. Drink lots of water. And, hey, by the way, did you get my message a while ago?"

"Yes. Did you really mean it?"

"Of course. Why not? I'll call you later."

He did, in three days, but she wasn't well yet. He told her she must go to the doctor; she declined, insisting there'd been improvement, that Mickey had brought her chicken soup, that her cough was nearly gone, that the sneezing was less. Once again Tad promised to call her in three days.

PAIR OF ACES arrived in the mail (Tad had no e-mail, no printer, no functioning computer -- the one he did have was missing an anti-virus security system, so he seldom used it). The role was intriguing -- "Jeff," a wanderer, picked up by fugitives, physical danger lurking, an existential adventure, a hint of romance with the female lead, a kiss, a look, a sad parting, the fugitives giving Tad's character money "for being a friend," the SUV speeding off, the sun setting, the character on the side of the highway, alone once more. Art! Not to mention, in between, an encounter with the crazed pursuers, a fight, a scramble to the SUV, a period of laughter and joy, New Mexico scenery flashing by. Tad deliberately avoided reading the film's climax, hoping that would help his performance, because his character <u>doesn't know</u> what happens. That way the knowledge of the ending wouldn't be in Tad's mind as he interacts (on film) with the other characters. Of course it may fail, this method, if someone mentions the ending to him at any time during filming -- an unfortunately predictable consequence of being on the set. But he intended -- plotted, really -- to request the others keep it a secret from him, if at all possible. His character doesn't know what's in store, ultimately, for the two lovers, after he sees them for the last time. Why should Tad?

So he started learning the lines while Franklin made the deal. First Tad read his part repeatedly, absorbing the scenes, the words, the reactions. Then, two days later, he began the arduous task of memorizing each line, each sentence, each phrase -- one phrase at a time, then one sentence at a time, and then each line, one at a time ("Lines" often contained more than one sentence, as in: "Hello. Where are you going?" Or "Want me to drive for a while? You look tired").

It would be interesting to work with Destiny, again, she was so fascinating, but Franklin indicated that was not a done deal, due to her initial reservations regarding the plot line and the nudity. But Tad wished she would give

in, take the money, and they could kiss outside the motel

room in the rain, as described in the script. No news on

who would play "Trask," the first-time drug connection who

chickens out and blows the deal. And shoots, wounding one

dealer, and runs. Lucky man, whoever he is, Tad thought,

getting to spend all that time with Destiny. Someday, of

course, Tad wanted a role like that.

One part he didn't care for -- the bad guys catch up

to them outside a restaurant and Trask gets to do all the

good stuff: punching, kicking, taking this gun from the

bag in the SUV, firing at the retreating figures, while Tad

recovers from a knockdown and Destiny runs to Trask's arms

gratefully. It didn't make Tad look like much of a hero.

There was an excellent scene by a campfire at night

where Tad's character (Jeff) has two long lines --

"speeches," really -- describing his past and his

existential outlook on life: creating one's own "being" in

one's own particular "situation." The lovers eat it up.

"Where did you get all that?" Sasha asks him. "Oh, here

and there, in books, I guess."

Franklin phoned -- he'd made the deal, angry the producers wouldn't pay more.

"I felt like telling them to bug off, but you need to think about the future. They might use you again sometime."

"Yeah. I like the role."

"I told them that, and they're lucky to get you so cheaply," Franklin said.

"Ten thousand ain't cheap to me!"

"Anyway, it'll have to be a whole lot more the next time they want you."

"You're a good man, Franklin."

"Well, congratulations. When I hear about the start date, I'll let you know. But plan on next month, for now. But if they shoot in continuity it could be a couple of months away."

"Cool. I'll be ready."

The time dragged on. He worried the movie wouldn't even happen, but at last a start date was confirmed.

Meanwhile, Tad dreamed he would someday own a classic car, a Chevy Malibu, and it would be of course absolutely <u>blue</u>. Now his Honda had to suffice. A blue Malibu would fit into his plans, would metaphysically bring him closer to the real thing, the real Malibu experience.

Rachel, the star of *WOMAN PAST AND PRESENT*, was on the news -- a new film coming out. "Good for her," he told himself. Someday perhaps he'd get a chance to work with her again. Why not?

Finally he got his computer set up with a new anti-virus security system, but Tad used it rarely. The internet didn't interest him. Frankly, only acting, cheeseburgers, and women interested him. Of course, there were women on the internet, but Tad preferred live ones, in stores, at the mall, or on the street, and at work (when he got any work). But Rachel hadn't expressed that subtle "interest" a woman can communicate; she'd cut short, in fact, between-take chitchat and stayed in her dressing room too much.

A cheeseburger, of course, didn't have to be interested in you, it only wanted eating, and acting, why, that you could do in your room, wandering around reading aloud from a book of poetry, or sitting on a park bench, repeating Shakespeare by heart. A woman needed care, needed warmth, needed excitement, needed presents, needed romance, needed physical attention -- even devotion.

Eating cheeseburgers was easier, for Tad, although since the therapy, sensuality was less "dangerous." The mixed-up stress and strain was less pronounced, the pain beneath the surface (Roy's attack) abated, the subconscious fear mostly gone. Sara had led him to sex tenderly, sensing his unspoken reluctance, and girls in college had wondered at Tad's moderate passion, his temperate desire. Until now Tad hadn't even noticed it, took it as normal, up until now (after the therapy), had barely recognized the difference between him and other men. Perhaps he'd call Margie to have another screaming session, perhaps he needed more "freeing." Perhaps he <u>would</u> talk to the police. He did know a few; one, in fact, who'd been in *ROUGH KIDS,* a sergeant with the Sheriff's Department. They'd spoken on set occasionally.

Tad got his phone number from the production company of *ROUGH KIDS*, arranged, nervously, a lunch, and told him everything. They were in a restaurant near the station.

The officer, Gilbert, after listening intently to Tad's story, said one word, emphatically: "Good." Tad could only respond, "Really?"

Gilbert told him not to worry about it, that he'd only been a kid at the time, that "cops have better things to do than hound someone who protected himself in such a way."

Naturally Tad picked up the check, enormously relieved, and Gilbert patted him on the back as they exited the restaurant.

Practicing for the role in *PAIR OF ACES*, Tad realized his acting was freer. He could see that. Acting required concentration and spontaneity, simultaneously -- deep concentration and brave spontaneity. The former he'd always been capable of, the latter only sporadically. Now, more open, Tad could let loose without as much fear. But there was still some, still some inner restriction -- yes, perhaps he would give Margie a call.

But instead he phoned Franklin to ask, particularly, if Destiny had accepted the part in *PAIR OF ACES*. She had, finally, after Franklin had coaxed her into it. But Tad didn't ask more, didn't say what was prompting him -- that he wanted to see her, go out with her. Tad couldn't bring himself to express those wishes. The therapy hadn't been <u>that</u> successful.

Destiny's main problem was the nudity, the "shower scene" in the motel. But in a sort of spirit of revenge, against Steve, had agreed to do it. Playing a waitress in

love with a ne'er-do-well appealed to her, but working on

out-of-the-way Arizona and New Mexico locations didn't.

But, "work was work," Hilda reminded her. Destiny studied

the script and exercised on a treadmill and ate salads,

angry at Steve, and hoping a movie star would fall madly in

love with her. Once, though, lying in bed late in the

evening, sleepless, staring at the ceiling, Destiny felt

weak, felt unsure of her big plan. A movie star, a

multimillion dollar earner, a tall (or short, who cared?)

celebrity might leave her as Steve had, disgusted with her

coldness, tired of her intellectual bent. Perhaps Destiny

was wrong, perhaps she ought to consider revising her

plans, find someone who truly cared about her, someone who

had more to offer than the glamour of pursuing paparazzi,

the Rolls-Royce, the credit-card access to Beverly Hills,

the Bel-Air mansion, the private jet. But, what would that

be? Honesty and love and partnership and a little

unpredictability? Well, she'd see, she'd wait, she'd see

who was set to play the lead opposite her, she'd give as

good a performance as she could, on film and off. She'd

think positive. Maybe that shower scene would cause a star

to seek her out -- although she doubted it. Her body
wasn't <u>that</u> great.

Destiny turned over, closing her eyes, tempted to pick
up again the book she'd been reading. But she didn't. She
stretched her arm out, she sighed softly, she held her
other hand between her thighs, and said, quietly, "Take me
with you, I'm bored with this job. I'm bored with this
existence." It was a line from the script.

Before leaving for the location Tad spent one night
with Faye, at her beach house. Faye seemed troubled, and
Tad questioned her. Dinner was on the patio, after sunset.
They sat at a small metal table covered by a white
tablecloth embroidered with red and blue curvy lines. The
maid served them, and Faye drank champagne, watching the
darkening horizon, only infrequently taking tiny bites of
food.

Tad stopped devouring his roasted chicken and potatoes
when he noticed how little she was eating.

"Is something wrong?" he asked bluntly.

She smiled at him. "Forgive me," she said. "You're a
young man, you can't know yet what it's like to be a good
deal past forty in a selfish, unfeeling world."

"I know the selfish, unfeeling part. Come on, eat."

She laughed and obeyed his command. Tad drank his beer, and waited, watching her valiant exertion with knife and fork. Faye would only pick up a piece of chicken with her fingers when the majority of its meat was gone.

"Good. Listen," he said. "You'll see, when I make it big, I'll get some great jobs for you, in every movie I make. Not everybody is selfish around here. I promise."

She only stared into his eyes.

"Really," he continued. "Don't lose hope. I'll make 'em write parts for you, and make 'em hire you. Not that I'll have to push all that hard. They'll want you. Definitely."

Faye looked away and sipped her champagne, whispering, "No, Tad, you will have to push them. But I'm grateful, so grateful for that sentiment."

"Is it a deal?" he asked. "You stop feeling bad and I'll get you a bunch of good parts. Okay?"

She put down her glass. "No, let's make the deal this way: you get me one good part, and then I'll stop feeling so bad."

"Oh no. Reverse it. On the strength of my promise, and not one role, only, you be happy, and when --"

She took his face in her hands, leaned over to kiss him, whispering afterward, "Alright. I'll be happy as of this moment." She wanted to add, "However things may turn out," but she didn't.

Finally Tad took a flight to Phoenix, then rode to the location silently, giving one or two word answers to the driver, gazing thoughtfully out the window at desert land, communities of tract houses, gas stations, ominous-looking complexes (military labs with alien bodies?), beautiful homes on rocky hills, and the endless western sky. He thought of the Louis L'Amour gunfighter novels he'd read, of secret hidden water holes, strong, faithful horses, blazing shootouts, weeping women, hard-faced lean riders, lonely campfires, Indians, bones in the sand.

At the motel in Apache Gap he took his bag to the lobby, questioning, suddenly, his ability to perform his part well, of getting along with the other actors, of even saying his lines convincingly. Doubts always burned in him before every job, but this time it was worse, for some reason. Partly he felt the pressure of doing well for Faye's sake, partly of tangling with Destiny, who somehow threatened him. Would she be cold? Would she be self-centered and egotistical, barely responding to his acting, only caring about how she came off, how she looked, how she controlled their scenes together? He'd worked with actresses like that previously, and dreaded the prospect now.

In his room Tad unpacked, drank water, lay morosely on the bed, ran over a few of his lines in his head, and napped.

The bright stars overhead that evening reminded Tad of the film's new title: *BRIGHT MOON*, but there was no moon to be found in the sky. He walked to a Burger King for food, purchased more water at the town's single gas station, and beer, and wandered back to his motel room. The second assistant director had called earlier, informing him a van would pick him up at 8 a.m. for a wardrobe consultation, and a courtesy trip to the set to meet the others. He had no scenes scheduled until the day after, but it was always beneficial to make contact with others in the cast, to take the edge off the discomfort of acting with strangers right off the bat. Of course he knew the director from *ROUGH KIDS*, and Destiny, slightly. Nevertheless, Roger Donicio, the handsome male lead, was a virtual mystery to Tad, aside from one movie, *STEPSON OF*

CASANOVA, a romantic comedy Tad had seen the year before. Roger had played the lead well, a smarmy lothario who wins hearts and bodies on his way to ultimate downfall at the hands of the vengeful, love-betrayed princess. Yet Roger was a star, of sorts, and Tad prepared himself for a large ego and a phony temperament. Not that Tad cared. He only wanted to do his part, get to know Destiny, and get out of there.

He slept well, awoke to the radio buzzing, showered and drank coffee until his ride arrived. The wardrobe meeting was brief -- how could he object to any of the costumer's choices? Tad tried everything on, a few alterations were recommended, and he went to the dirt road back-country location to meet Roger and Destiny, and the director, again. Everything went well, actually. Roger was more friendly than expected, Destiny was cool and exquisite, Gregory was enthusiastic and rushed.

He watched the instant scene being rehearsed and filmed near the SUV, Roger's character assuring Destiny's they would survive this "ordeal." The two of them gazing tiredly at the desert, taking sips from a shared Aquafina bottle, Roger's character firing a pistol shot at a relatively close rock, handing the pistol to "Sasha," to

"try it, will you?" She declined, "afraid of guns"; he
insisted, "you must, really." She did, missing the rock,
laughing, trying again, missing again.

"I couldn't possibly shoot anyone," she said. "You'll
have to protect us both."

"Trask" took the gun and kissed her, saying, rather
meekly, Tad thought, "I will."

"Cut," Gregory boomed. "Once more."

Why they changed the title from *PAIR OF ACES* to *BRIGHT
MOON* Tad didn't know, but during his ride back to the motel
he considered the possibility they feared a critic calling
it *PAIR OF ASSES* in a review. Tad chuckled but said
nothing when the driver asked him what was so funny.

That evening he looked over his lines. It was the big
action sequence at the roadside restaurant. Tad only had
to say a few short lines -- the others, including the drug
dealers, had most of the dialogue. But he repeated "What's
this all about?" and "Relax, dipshit," and "Who were those
guys, anyway?" over and over, drinking beer, visualizing
the fight, and recalling *BUTCH CASSIDY AND THE SUNDANCE
KID*.

The morning, at the location, was fun. Destiny was in good spirits, Gregory liked action, to direct, and Roger had a gleam of excitement in his eyes. The trailers and crew trucks were parked behind the roadside restaurant, out of camera range, the scene was to be "day for day" (story-wise daytime, filmed during the day) which made lighting easier, since the weather was clear, although hot.

The call sheet said "having had," meaning Tad reported to work having had breakfast, which he got from a diner near the Apache Gap gas station, and coffee was available on the set for everyone, as usual, and water and soda and bags of chips and cookies.

Tad went to "hair and makeup," put on his hitchhiker clothes (shabby), and stood near the mobile dressing-room wagon, talking to two of the extras. Their job was to be in the parking lot during the confrontation. There were four male actors playing the pursuing bad guys; they kept to themselves near the coffee dispenser.

Lighting and camera equipment was already being set up when Tad arrived, and Gregory had described to the stunt people (all men, since Destiny had no difficult fighting to do -- only once a bad guy was supposed to grab at her but release his grip when "Trask" hit him and kicked him) all of the basic action. Even the crew members appeared enthusiastic, unlike their normal attitude of the day before. Prop department had guns ready, the stuntmen were dressed like Roger and two of the bad guys, the SUV was parked in place, a surreptitiously lit restaurant window revealed wooden tables and a waitress/extra inside, dressed for duty.

Roger, Destiny and Tad were to exit the restaurant, after supposedly eating, to be accosted by three of the drug dealers who had followed them to the "New Mexico" location (although it was actually Arizona). After an exchange of angry words, but no guns drawn (too public for that) the bad guys demanded money. Originally "Trask's" zipper bag with his pistol was to be in the SUV, but he suggested and Gregory agreed, he'd have it with him in the restaurant. So that made it more convenient (and realistic) that he could pull his gun and fire, and Tad and Destiny would duck and drop to the ground as Roger continued to stand, and fire. The bad guys fled to their car (a driver within, waiting), raced away, "Trask" running but not shooting again.

Roger and Gregory held a heated discussion, Roger not wanting to punch or kick anyone, and finally Gregory agreed to leave that out.

Simple, but it would take half of the day to film. First off, Tad would be filmed exiting the restaurant ahead of Roger and Destiny, see the waiting thugs, and be pushed around by "Drake," the biggest one. That's where he said, "What's this all about?" Roger would say a line, behind him, and Destiny would add to it. The camera was on Tad and the bad guys during rehearsal. Gregory gave him no instructions. It was his first scene in the schedule, but Tad had to feel like he'd been riding with "Trask and Sasha" for 24 hours.

Destiny looked good in her jeans and low-cut top. She surprised Tad by touching his shoulder from behind. When he turned to see her she said, rather formally, "Good morning." He repeated the same to her.

"Are you ready to be punched in the face?" she asked, informally.

"Why, yes, I think so," he replied, more formally than he'd planned. She smiled, nodded at the extras, and walked away toward her dressing room. She wasn't flirting with him, she only wanted to get him on her side, to keep the mood light. Roger had been overly serious, in her estimation, and Destiny wanted to break that spell. Perhaps a little attention from Tad would do the trick. Lurking in her mind was the continuing hope of marrying a star, and Roger, while not exactly qualifying, had potential.

"Okay, everyone," Gregory announced, "let's try it."

The first a.d. organized the first rehearsal, Roger came from his dressing room, the camera crew watched, the actors went into the restaurant, the 'bad guys' waited outside.

"Action!" Gregory yelled.

Tad came out, thinking: I just ate, I feel good, I don't expect anything.

The bad guys stepped from behind the camera -- a threatening group. Tad began to walk around them but the big one pushed him back. "Hold it, pal," he said.

"What's this all about?" Tad asked, as "Jeff."

And so it proceeded, Roger and Destiny speaking to the big guy, calling him "Drake," Tad trying to act as though this surprised him, but not too much -- he wanted to play coolness in his character's approach to the world. As "Drake" got worked up, Tad said "Relax, dipshit," and Drake threw a wide "punch," Tad dropped to the ground, Roger and Destiny ran forward, "Drake" lunged suddenly at Destiny, she jumped backward, Roger pulled his gun from his zipper bag, the bad men retreated, and turned, and ran, off-camera, flinging epithets, and Gregory yelled "Cut! Good. Let's get that punch right. Spike?" He looked around him and Spike, the stunt coordinator, dressed as a bad guy, approached. "What about it?" Gregory asked him. Tad, standing now, edged closer to listen to the stuntman.

They arranged the punch, and fall, and Spike seemed satisfied. Tad glanced at Destiny, who was now sitting in a chair near the restaurant door in the shade. She wasn't interested in anything, it appeared. Roger had gone inside, to sit down, also. He, oddly, didn't appear interested in Destiny.

By two p.m., after a break for lunch, it was all done, including gunshots fired by "Trask" into the air over the fleeing men, and one shot from them (missing) as they sped away, and "Jeff's" question, "Who were those guys, anyway?" unanswered by a stoic Trask -- all except the final part where the three travelers leap into their SUV, Trask driving (of course), madly attempting to avoid further contact with the bad guys and a resultant police investigation. While the crew worked to set up for that scene, Tad relaxed in a chair, Roger in his dressing room, and Destiny inside the restaurant, now, talking on her cell phone to Hilda.

Tad wondered, but said nothing, about the theoretical possibility a "bystander" might have gotten the SUV's license plate number and told the police, causing a glitch in the three escapees' escape. But he didn't want to cause trouble. Details like that were generally skipped over in low-budget films. It could be assumed no one took down the license plate number, and the SUV's description was too vague for the police to apprehend anyone later, on the road -- including the bad guys' vehicle, going the other direction. If the critics later faulted it as implausible, so be it.

He drank Sprite, he thought about Destiny. She ate potato chips, speaking to Hilda about Roger's failure to approach her, to make even the slightest effort at seduction, and how she wished the job was over. Roger slept in his trailer, oblivious to the activity around him, romantic or otherwise.

The way Roger ran the SUV out of the parking lot, later, with Destiny and Tad swaying violently sideways, led Tad to believe Roger was on cocaine. But, in fact, that wasn't the case. He'd only had coffee prior to the scene and wanted to act as macho as possible, to impress the audience.

Destiny complained about his driving before the next take, and Roger (resentfully) slowed it down a bit. The director and the cinematographer were happy, so Tad was released for the day. The others had to film the beginning of the sequence, the SUV driving into the parking lot, but Spike would take Tad's place in the back seat, wearing Tad's shirt. There was also a twilight "driving" shot to film, so the crew loaded equipment, preparing to move to another spot up the highway. Tad said goodbye to Destiny, who didn't give him a hug, of course, but did smile and remark, "You're good, Tad. I'm happy we finally got together again. See you tomorrow?"

"Yes. You're good too."

"Thanks. Want to go over some lines tomorrow? I'll ask Roger if he can."

"Sure. Great. Anytime. See you."

"'Bye."

He left, a sharp sadness in his heart. It was due to the knowledge Roger was playing the lead, and Tad wasn't. But he was also excited to be in <u>any</u> scenes with her. She had something... indefinable, graceful... something, and she wasn't self-centered, as he'd feared.

After filming the SUV's entrance, and the highway driving shot, which story-wise takes place before they pick up the hitchhiker Jeff, Destiny and Roger returned to their dressing rooms, changed out of wardrobe, initialed the sign-out sheet, ate dinner together at the very restaurant which had served as the "New Mexico" shootout location, and discussed, professionally, the next day's work.

Roger drank whiskey, Destiny, wine. He spoke of his girlfriend, a fashion model, and Destiny's heart sank. To her inquiry about whether they planned to marry, Roger said "Yes, definitely."

Riding to the motel Destiny grieved a little, gave up on Roger, looked toward the future, and prayed a prayer to Jesus. Maybe she'd see if Tad was single -- he seemed to like her.

Tad, for his part, was more intrigued than ever. After a shower and a beer he had walked to the diner, feeling the evening air against his face, deciding boldly to approach her, some way or other, come what may. By the time he'd finished eating, and had another beer, his plan was firmly in place.

Destiny, riding in the car from location, in the back seat with Roger, thought to herself: I'll just see what happens. If Tad becomes a star, great. If not, I'll re-evaluate. And if I fall in love with him, what does it matter? She looked out the window and saw at the beginning of the Eisenhower era at the beginning of the Eisenhower era the moon rising. A bright one.

Printed in Great Britain
by Amazon